KAREN LEIBY BELLI

iUniverse®

THE GHOST FROM THE STAINED GLASS WINDOW

iUniverse books may be ordered through booksellers or by contacting:

iUniverse
1663 Liberty Drive
Bloomington, IN 47403
www.iuniverse.com
1-800-Authors (1-800-288-4677)

Because of the dynamic nature of the Internet, any web addresses or links contained in this book may have changed since publication and may no longer be valid. The views expressed in this work are solely those of the author and do not necessarily reflect the views of the publisher, and the publisher hereby disclaims any responsibility for them.

Any people depicted in stock imagery provided by Getty Images are models, and such images are being used for illustrative purposes only.
Certain stock imagery © Getty Images.

ISBN: 978-1-5320-8726-4 (sc)
ISBN: 978-1-5320-8728-8 (hc)
ISBN: 978-1-5320-8727-1 (e)

Library of Congress Control Number: 2020910426

Print information available on the last page.

iUniverse rev. date: 06/08/2020

To Larry, my husband,
best friend, and the love of my life

For Jonny, Matthew, and Adam,
my inspirations

CHAPTER 1

Mysterious Whispers

It was almost 7:00 a.m. on a Saturday. At last, the massive doors thundered open for the morning preview. It would be two hours until the official auction time. A huge bear of a man stood by the opening. Twelve-year-old Dani Roberson stuffed her cell back in her pocket, swished her long brown hair aside, and entered.

"Good morning, missy." His appealing Irish brogue brought an instant smile to Dani's face.

"Hi, Liam."

"You're first in line, I see. And that's a *first* for you after all these years. You must have found something mighty important last night." He winked and stood aside for Dani and the small crowd that waited.

Friday night was the normal preview. She whisked past him and into the building, too excited to answer. She would normally stand and talk to Liam because he told her jokes and made her feel welcome in this mostly adult environment. She always looked forward to the monthly event, but this one was different.

Whiffs of old wood, musty oriental rugs, and ancient book smells reached her nose. The pleasant aroma of hot dogs grilling made her stomach growl. *Should have eaten breakfast.*

She loved the excitement of the auction. But this time there was something specific she wanted—or it wanted her. Had it not whispered to her, she never would have found it.

"Wait up," her dad, Ray Roberson, called. Towering about six feet tall with sandy brown hair, he was very handsome.

She turned to find them out of breath, trying to catch up. They had insisted on waiting in the car, drinking their coffee. Amused, Dani watched as her mom, thirty-nine-year-old Regina Roberson, turned sideways and squeezed down an aisle of Persian rugs piled high on antique chests. Her green eyes, long brown hair, and perpetual smile endeared her to most of the people she met. *She's as slender as a magazine model,* Dani thought. Looking at her now, Dani realized how proud she was of both her parents.

Dad laughed. "You *are* on a mission, aren't you?"

"I just want to get to it before anyone else does." Making a face, Dani continued down aisle after aisle packed with old chairs, lamps, and you name it, until she came to the stained glass window. It stood about four feet high. She gazed at it, mesmerized. Although it was dusty and corroded with what looked like decades of dirt on the bottom, the appeal of the colors in the stained glass was breathtaking. Even here, hidden from sunlight, it sparkled.

Her mother called after her. "Dani, this is a rather huge piece. Where would we put it?"

"Really, Mom? It will be perfect in my bedroom. The sun will shine right through it and make my whole room reflect like a crystal."

"It seems a little morbid, sweetheart, like something that belongs in an old church, not a young girl's bedroom. Perhaps there's another stained glass window that would be cheerier looking."

"It's not that bad, Mom. It's just dusty from sitting here," Dani said, trying to sound authoritative.

Mom smiled. "This thing is at least two feet wide, and it's almost as tall as you are."

"It's good-quality wood, very old but holding up nicely." Dad ran his hands over the stained glass window and then looked at his wife for agreement.

"Of course it's beautiful, Dani. I can see why you're attracted to it. But maybe there's another piece here that's a more suitable size and perhaps not from a church. There are many different stained glass pieces. Let's see if there's another one nearby."

This is ludicrous. I want that glass window, Dani thought.

"We don't even know if we'll get it. We do have to bid on it first," her dad remarked.

He's on my side. I can tell. Being an only child meant that Dani's parents doted on her, but there were limits. They usually didn't take her side against each other. They stuck together on most decisions involving her. This was rare that her dad was actually supportive of purchasing the piece.

Dani thought there was something about this particular piece. Last night at the preview, it had lured her. There wasn't any light on it, tucked away as it was, but there was a gleam emanating from it, not to mention whispers—at least she thought so.

As if reading her mind, her mom asked, "How did you ever find it way back here, hidden behind a ton of rugs and other stuff?"

Dani frowned, ignoring her. She continued pleading her case, focusing on her dad.

"I want to hang it in one of the windows in my room. The pink and yellow in the rectangle panes with the deep purple flower in the middle will be gorgeous when the sun shines through them. I have two hundred dollars. I'll pay for it if you'll just bid on it for me. Please, Dad."

Her dad's response sounded like a stall for time. "I'd like to have Brett take a look at it, see if he has any provenance on it before we do anything." He gave her mom a weak smile.

"Provenance? Really? I don't care where it came from. I love it."

Dani had been coming to Anderson Auction since she was in diapers, so she was well aware of what the term *provenance* meant and why it was important to collectors. But she didn't really care where it originated from or all the places it had been. She had to have this stained glass window.

"We aren't stained glass collectors. I only care about this one." She surprised herself at how strongly she spoke to her parents. What made her so obstinate?

As it turned out, Brett, the auctioneer, wasn't very helpful, his job being to offer each piece for auction, call for people to bid money on it, and then award it to the highest bidder. The auctioneer was usually familiar with where it came from too.

"I can't tell you where it's been. We got it from an old salvage yard in Upper Bucks County," he said. "Sat there for decades. The property was sold, and all the contents came to auction. I'm surprised you found it. It was hidden behind a lot of junk."

"I don't care about all that," Dani piped up. "I want it."

"I've never heard you be so adamant, Dani." Brett chuckled.

"Or so rude, young lady," her mom said.

"I'm sorry. It's very pretty, and it would look great in my room. That's all."

Dani surprised herself. But that wasn't all. *There's something weird about this piece. Why do I have to have it?*

She reviewed the events of Friday night in her mind as she ran her hand over the glass. Touching it, she felt it tingle beneath her fingers. Startled, she pulled back. Glancing at the adults, she observed that luckily no one had noticed her sudden movement.

Dad's voice interrupted her thoughts. "Your mom and I have discussed it, Dani. If you want the stained glass window and are willing to pay for it and clean it up, we'll bid on it for you."

"Brett says he doesn't think it will pull more than a hundred dollars so you're in luck," Mom said in a monotone voice.

"Oh, really, guys? You're the best. You won't regret it, Mom. You'll see how gorgeous it will look." Dani hugged them both, her dad laughing and her mom expressionless.

Her parents wandered around the place until the bidding started. Dani stayed close to the stained glass window, following men employed by the auction house as they carried it up on the dais, where they moved it for bidding. It was among the first items, along with crystal and various lamps. The glass sparkled, sending out tiny diamond-shape sparks from its spot on the stage.

Dani shivered. It was dim in the room, void of any strong lighting on the glass. She glanced at her parents, but they didn't seem to be seeing what she was witnessing.

The bidding started, and Dad was the only bidder. Dani was ecstatic, already picturing it over the center window in her room. Everything was going well, but then a man chimed in from nowhere, and the bidding was up over two hundred dollars within seconds.

"I'm sorry, honey. I tried. We went up to three hundred dollars. I'm afraid we lost it." Her dad reached for her and hugged her.

She was shocked. She had been so sure of getting it. "It's okay, guys. Thanks. You tried."

A sigh of relief escaped her mom. "We're going to stay a few moments and see what happens with some of the art. Why don't you get yourself a funnel cake?"

"No thanks, Mom. I'll sit over here and wait for you." Without looking at them, she moped over to an empty chair. Looking back at the platform, she watched as the men carted off the stained glass window. Tiny flashes of light sprang from it like a circle of vibrant fireflies. The men carrying it off the stage didn't seem to notice anything unusual.

I can't believe that I lost that piece. I have to find a way to get it. She looked all around the auction house, trying to think of a way to get the piece. She twisted her long brown hair around her finger, waiting and thinking. Then ...

That's the buyer! Summoning up courage that she didn't know she had, she approached him.

"Excuse me. I noticed you just bid on that stained glass window."

"Why, yes, I did, young lady."

"Well, I noticed a more expensive but even more beautiful piece right around this corner." Dani led the surprised man down an aisle to a magnificent stained glass window.

"My, I didn't see this before. You're correct, little lady. It beats the one I bid on."

"I'm willing to pay you one hundred dollars for it. I really have to have it. It was in my family for years, and suddenly my grandparents passed and it was lost." Dani knew it was a long shot, but she was relying on the fact that the man looked wealthy in his three-piece suit and that he would be taken by the charm she was using on him. "Please, mister, I would really appreciate your kindness and understanding." *I hate myself for doing this— but not a lot.*

"Well, since I would rather have the other stained glass piece and since you presented your case so sweetly, little lady, I will make your deal. Let's go over to the clerk and fill out the paperwork. We'll have to get a parent to sign for you, though."

Dani was so pleased and excited that she didn't even worry about how she was going to present this to her parents.

"Mom, Dad, this gentleman agreed to sell me the stained glass window." Dani took her dad by the hand and dragged him to the clerk booth. The man had already signed the transfer. Dad just had to fill in the names.

"Um, this is very kind of you, sir. What did you say your name was?" Dad asked, running his hand through his hair with a confused look.

"IH is the moniker I go by." He shook hands with her mom and dad, winked at Dani, and left.

Dani whooped and hugged them. Then she stopped. Out of the corner of her eye, she saw the stained glass window standing next to the cashier's booth. A faint greenish glow emanated from it. She tried to suppress the fear that engulfed her, but her whole body shuddered involuntarily. The happiness she felt moments ago was replaced by an unknown fear. After loading the window into the Jeep, they drove home.

"I appreciate you two doing the grocery shopping," her mom said when they got home. "I made this hair appointment, and I really need a trim. I hate it when my hair gets this long."

"I think you look great, Mom."

"Ditto for me." Dad smiled. "But we're happy to do it. We'll take the Camry. We can unload the piece later."

They went their separate ways. Dani and her dad returned an hour and a half later to an empty house.

"Regina? Hmm, maybe she went shopping. It's hard for her

to pass Marshalls without stopping in." Her dad smiled at Dani, who winked back.

They were unpacking food when the doorbell rang. "Yes?" Dani was startled to find two uniformed police officers at the door.

"May we speak to your dad?" They were so serious and soft-spoken that they caused Dani to shiver.

"Yes, come in. D-dad?" she stuttered, starting to sense something bad.

"Can we talk in private for a minute?" they asked him.

"Oh, yes. Dani, will you go finish putting away the groceries, please?"

Dani strained to hear the conversation from behind the kitchen doors. The next words were horrific. The officers explained that her mom had been hit head-on and was killed immediately. The car was demolished.

CHAPTER 2

Spiders and a Ouija Board

B ucket in one hand, roll of paper towels tucked underneath her armpit, and cleaning solution in the other hand, Dani trudged to the basement with Riley, her golden retriever, bouncing behind.

It would soon be a year since she had first acquired the stained glass window. She shuddered. The events that followed that day had prevented her from cleaning or hanging it. Ironically, it was the only thing that had remained intact after the car crash. The car had been totaled, and they'd stored the window in the basement. She moved to the area housing the stained glass window and carefully removed the quilt covering it. Riley sniffed and snarled at it, backing away immediately.

"Ri, what is it buddy?" A huge black spider sprang from the glass. Dani dropped her cleaning supplies and screamed. Two more sprang from the glass, then three, then an entire nest, and they kept coming. Working her finger on the button of the glass cleaner, which was the only remotely potent thing in her hand, she tried to kill them, but to no avail. They kept spewing out of the glass.

"They won't stop, Riley."

Riley pounced on as many as he could, barking and snarling at them. Suddenly, they were gone as quickly as they had appeared.

Sneakers plodding down the staircase belonged to her dad. "What are you screaming at?"

Every bone in her body seemed to shake as she made her way to his arms. "Dad, I was cleaning the glass, and a million spiders came out of it. They were everywhere." He put his arms around her and surveyed the basement. Riley whined and inched closer to him. Her dad's arms and body felt so much thinner. He had lost weight in the year since her mom passed, and his thinning sandy brown hair was showing wisps of white around his temples.

"Where are they now?" Still holding her, he extended his hand, moving about the area. "There aren't any spiders, honey." His voice sounded gentle, as if he didn't believe her.

Riley growled, backing away from the stained glass window, validating Dani's words.

"Sp-sp-spiders, big black ones everywhere, Dad." She was sobbing as she hugged him.

"Dani, look, there's nothing, honey." Her dad sighed, tightening his arms around her. "Maybe there were a few and you killed them? We both know how much you hate spiders. And I can see how this stained glass window may bring some memories and emotions. After all, the last time you saw it ... Well, let's forget it right now, okay? Come upstairs and we'll talk and rest. How about if I pack up some things in the den and you can lie on the couch and talk to me?"

They were preparing to sell the house and move to a rental property nearby. On top of all their troubles in the last year, Dad had lost his job. His architectural engineering firm had to downsize. Dani had volunteered to start packing up things in the basement, and the stained glass window came to mind first. She couldn't explain why.

Tingles ran down her back. This thing hadn't been out of the closet an hour and weird things were happening again. She did remember how her mom felt about it, and now her mom was dead. She watched as her dad packed some books.

"I miss Mommy." She cried for the first time since her mom had died. Her dad sat beside her and hugged her.

"Honey, I can't imagine what you're going through. I miss her too." They sat together without speaking for some time. Then, blowing her nose, Dani sat up.

"I'm okay now, Dad. You might be right. The stained glass window has been in storage since we bought it. Seeing it ..."

"I know. Things will get better. It'll just take more time. I have to insist that you not go near that piece alone again. We'll clean and pack it together or I'll do it myself. You, young lady, stay out of the basement." He hugged her. "Let me go through these boxes and we'll call it quits for the day."

Dani watched as he pulled a box down from a shelf. The lid slid off and cards, charts, and old papers fell out.

"Oh, here, I'll help."

"No, Dani," her father shouted too quickly. He scooped everything together and threw it back in the box. "I'm sorry I shouted. I don't want you to get your hands dusty on this old junk."

Dani eyed him. He'd never displayed *that* behavior before. *I wonder what that was all about.*

"Tell you what—let's play with Riley for a while outside. It's a nice day, and we all can use the exercise."

"Sounds good, Dad."

They went outside and threw a ball around with the golden retriever for about an hour.

The fun-loving dog grabbed the ball and ran off into the small wooded area outside the common ground near the town house. "Riley, get back here!" her dad called.

Laughing, Dani said, "I'll get him." She ran off after the ball and the dog. Entering the woods, she stopped cold. The woods became icy, and the wind whipped up.

"Riley, Riley!" she called to him. She then saw him staring at a filmy apparition of a bulldog. Suddenly, the specter was gone and the calm and warmth returned to the woods.

I'm not telling Dad about this. Shaking, she tried to regain her composure as she grabbed Riley, ball in mouth, and led him from the woods.

"Dani, you're shivering and your eyes are tearing up. I hope you're not coming down with something."

She hugged him. "I do feel a little feverish. Can we go home now?"

The next morning, she awoke in a good mood, having almost forgotten the events of the day before. She dressed to the sun pouring through her window and romped down the stairs with Riley by her side.

"Hey, there she is." Her dad was pouring juice for her and getting a yogurt from the fridge. "I have to leave in a few. Think you can hang out with Ri for a while? I'll only be a couple of hours."

Ordinarily, she wouldn't have hesitated, but today she didn't want her dad to go anywhere.

"Why? I want you to stay home with me today. It's the last week of summer, and I want you to spend time with me," she whined. This was out of the ordinary for the usually strong-minded Dani. *I hate myself for acting like a two-year-old. It's not my style, but ...* She thought about the spiders.

"Dani, I have an interview I can't miss. This job is important for us. It will be quick, and then I'll be home and the rest of the day is ours."

She knew how important it was. He had told her all about it in detail. He was the youngest person in his firm, with the least amount of years. They were giving him three months' severance pay, but that wouldn't cover their expenses. Jobs in his field were hard to find. She could repeat the mantra she had heard so many times now.

"Dad, I just didn't want to be alone today."

"You aren't alone. Mrs. Olsen is right next door."

"I don't care." In tears, she ran to the couch in the living room.

"Look, honey, it's just a couple of hours. I have to go." He tried to hug her, but she shoved him away. "I promise I'll be as quick as I can. You have Mrs. Olsen's cell number."

Dani watched as he glanced back at her and went out the door with a sad frown. She hated herself for making him feel bad. He was under enough stress, but she couldn't stop herself.

Grabbing Riley, she pulled him to the couch. She moped in silence for several minutes. "Ri, I'm acting like a little kid." Riley looked at her and turned his head in question. "I'm thirteen, and I should act it." Riley whined. "You're supposed to be on my side. Let's go clean that piece and pack up some things in the basement. I was so upset when I first saw it; I guess because it reminded me of Mom. Your mind *can* play tricks on you. I probably imagined those spiders." She sprang off the couch and headed for the basement door. Riley whimpered.

"Oh, come on, chicken." Laughing, she bolted down the stairs.

She hummed, filling the bucket with hot soapy water. The ringing of her iPhone stopped her.

"Madisen. Hey. No, I'm confined to the house. Not really *confined*, but my dad has an interview so he isn't here to drive me anywhere. And I really feel like I should help him pack for the move, especially because I was so awful to him this morning."

Dani wanted Madisen to come over, and she didn't think her dad would be that upset. The rule used to be that an adult had to be present if she was at anyone's house or if she had friends over, but that was before … There didn't seem to be any rules now. And she could tell her about the weird things that were happening. She and Dani had met in Little People Day Care. They graduated from kindergarten there and were still best friends.

Several minutes later, Madisen's mom's BMW arrived in the driveway. Dani ran out to meet them.

"Hi, Mrs. C. Thanks for bringing Madisen over."

"You're very welcome, Dani. Have fun." They waved as she pulled out.

"I'm glad she didn't ask to see my dad. I hate lying."

"She couldn't care less." Madisen's dark red hair shone in the sunlight as she patted Dani's hand. "I love my mom, but she's not warm and fuzzy. She's sort of void of emotion."

"I'm sure that's not true. You're lucky you have her."

"I'm sorry. I didn't mean it. I guess I led her to think that your dad was here."

"Well, I'm trying to help him pack. Maybe if we clean up the stained glass and get the basement started, he'll overlook your being here." Dani wasn't sure what to expect, but she didn't feel as scared with Madisen there. She was eager to confide her experiences with the stained glass window. They told each other everything.

As the girls gathered their cleaning and packing supplies, Dani filled Madisen in on some of the details. "At the auction last year, I was *pulled* to this stained glass window. I could hear it somehow whispering. And I had this weird feeling. It, like, engulfed me. I can't explain it. I was so drawn to it, like I was paralyzed."

"That's unbelievable, Dani. Why didn't you tell me before this?"

"My mom, well, she died right after. We didn't hang it. My dad put it in the closet down here." Dani kept waiting for some weird action from the glass but got nothing.

"It's not doing anything now," Madisen noted.

"I know. I see that." Dani wasn't sure if she was relieved or disappointed. They polished the glass with cleaner, and it shone brighter, even in the dim basement. Dani scrubbed the bottom where an inscription was, but it was so corroded that the dirt didn't budge.

"What do you think the writing says?" Madisen asked.

"I have no idea. My mom didn't care for it."

"It's beautiful, Dani. It looks very old, but it still gleams like a new piece of glass. Except this part." She pointed to the crusty section of caked-on dirt at the bottom. "Too bad we can't get that clean."

"That's the best we can do. Let's leave it for now. Can you help me throw out or box up this closet of stuff over here? Then I'll treat for ice cream. Dad left some money, and we can walk to the corner." Dani's face was pleading.

"Awesome."

They rooted through box after box, throwing out old dilapidated Halloween costumes and worn- decorations. "Dad won't want these." Dani pulled out a black and dark green plastic thing with a plug. "Look at this!" She held it up for Madison.

"I remember this thing. It's the gargoyle your dad used to plug in and scare us with when we were younger."

"I'm keeping this." Dani laughed. "I doubt that we'll be decorating for Halloween this year, so this will be our only piece." She put the dusty object on the table of things to go upstairs.

Madisen was pulling a rectangular object from the top shelf way back in the closet. "What's this, Dani? Wow, it's a Ouija board. You never told me you had one." Madisen gave her a questioning look.

"Because I didn't know we did." While sliding the board out, a yellowed piece of paper slipped from the box with a phrase scribbled in ink. "'Twelve Ouija Board Rules,'" it says. "This looks like my mom's handwriting."

"Let's read the rules," Madisen said.

"Number one is don't ever taunt a spirit." The girls looked at each other and giggled.

"Two," Dani read, "be careful with the questions you ask."

"What does that mean?" Madisen raised her eyebrows.

"It says you can't ask a question you don't want to know the answer to, like when you're going to die."

"Oh, guess not."

"Your turn."

"Not all spirits tell the truth." Madisen gasped.

"Number four, never use a Ouija board alone. Don't worry. I'm scared even with you here."

"Let's practice." Dani suggested. "Are there any spirits here?" She placed her hands on the planchette and it moved to *yes*. "Oh!" Dani screamed.

"Let me." Madisen grabbed the board and moved the planchette. "Who are you?" It spelled out the word *glass*.

A car door slamming caused the girls to stop.

"That's my dad. Don't tell him I told you anything about the piece. He doesn't believe me, and he'd be furious. Quick—help me hide this." Dani looked around for a place to store the Ouija board. "We can get it later." I don't think he would be happy if he knew I found this, because he's not a big fan of the supernatural." Dani didn't realize that when she put the board back in the box, she'd left the planchette on top of the board. That was rule number eight.

"No problem."

Seconds later, he called, "Dani, where are you?"

"Down here, Dad. Madisen came over. She's helping me. We're packing up stuff and throwing stuff out."

He joined them. "Hey, Madisen. Glad to see you, girl." He high-fived her and then turned to Dani. "I thought we agreed no basement."

Dani could tell he was keeping his anger in check. If Madisen weren't here, he would be shouting and lecturing because she disobeyed him. He wasn't as patient as he used to be.

"Dad, I'm sorry. It was stupid yesterday. I was upset, but I'm fine now. We cleaned the glass too, with no issues." She hugged him.

Her dad surveyed the stained glass window. "Nice job." He bent down and looked closely at the bottom. "Too bad we don't know more about it. Bet it has a good story to tell. I'd like to see what that inscription says." He stood up and faced them, hands on hips. "Thanks, ladies. I'll take it upstairs. We can store it with the stuff we're taking in the small van, not in the big moving van." He picked it up and climbed the stairs.

When the basement door closed, Madisen said, "Wow, your dad didn't even say anything about my being here." Madisen hugged her.

"I think he was happy you were here and there were no *incidents* with the stained glass window." Dani was relieved. "But what do you think? Do you believe the board? I'm still shaking. What do you think that meant?"

"You know it meant that the spirit and the stained glass window are connected, Dani. Don't go near that piece and don't use that board again without me."

The girls hung out talking about the beginning of school and trying not to talk about the Ouija. Then her dad took them for ice cream and drove Madisen home.

"I hope you can come over soon, Madisen," Dani whispered as she hugged her goodbye. "We need to learn how to use that Ouija."

"Great," Madisen replied, running to her front door. Dani wasn't sure if she meant it facetiously.

Her dad didn't mention a thing on the ride home about her disobeying him. Instead, he said, "I'm glad you and Madisen are friends. She's a really nice kid."

"Yup, my best friend. Dad, do you know anything about Ouija boards?

She thought her dad's face frowned.

"Why?"

"I found one in a closet in the basement. I didn't know we had one. It looks like mom's handwriting on a list of rules she wrote. Did Mom have one? You know, maybe when she was a teenager?" She hoped her father would admit that her mom owned one.

"No, can't say that she did. I never saw one." He changed the conversation to dinner and didn't mention it for the rest of the night.

After dinner, they watched a sitcom they both liked.

"Dad, why are you laughing? That isn't even funny." Dani

laughed at him. She was happy right now that they were sitting on the couch with Riley, snuggled up together.

"You may not find the humor in it, but I do." He laughed some more. "Must be an adult thing."

"Or a guy thing." Dani smirked but smiled to herself. *That's okay.* Then she said, "I'm going up to read before bedtime, okay?"

"Sounds good. In about an hour, I'll be up to tuck you in."

She and Riley headed upstairs. Dani opened her door and gulped. The Ouija board was on the floor in front of her. "What? Oh my God. Riley, how did this get here? We did put it away, didn't we?"

The planchette moved to spell out *no.*

Dani froze. Suddenly, the lights went out in her room and the moonlight cast the shadow of a bulldog on her bedroom wall.

CHAPTER 3

Shadow of a Tombstone

She ran to the window and peered out. The wind was howling, and rain was pouring down. The poor dog was whimpering and sopping wet. She ran out of her room and down the stairs, Riley behind her. The lights were on in the rest of the house.

Pulling open the front door, Dani stepped outside. Her heart was beating rapidly in her chest. Riley wagged his tail furiously and sniffed.

"If there *was* a bulldog Riley, he couldn't have gone very far. They don't move that fast." Tightening her robe around her, she stepped onto the grass and walked to the edge of the driveway.

Riley jumped off the step. His expert sense of smell left him circling in bewilderment.

"The grass is dry. No sign of any rainstorm." Dani gave an involuntary shiver. "Let's go back inside and deal with the Ouija board. Closing the door, she turned to face the stained glass window, which was standing against the entryway wall void of all its quilt wrappings.

"Dani, what are doing down here? I thought you went to read." Her dad wrinkled his brow.

Dani's arm shook as she pointed to the stained glass window.

"Why did you put it here? I thought we had it all packed up." He picked it up and moved it back to the den closet. Dani stood there clutching her body. "What were you thinking?" He called to her. "Come in here."

Dani walked toward the den. "Dad, I didn't put it there." Her face was furrowed in fear.

"Honey, it didn't just walk there by itself. I don't know what's up with you, but I do know it's just me and you and Riley in this house. Let's sit here for a minute. He waited a few seconds before he asked, "Do you want to talk about anything, honey?"

"Dad, I don't know. I can't explain. I feel strange. All of a sudden, there was a bulldog, sopping wet, looking in through the glass in the living room door. Riley saw it too." She darted a look at the retriever, who moaned and slunk down in response. "It was pouring, and when I opened the door, it was gone and there wasn't any sign of a dog or a storm. And the stained glass window ..." She stopped, and tears welled up in her eyes.

Her dad hugged her. "Look, maybe we should see Dr. Robin. Maybe you can talk to her about your feelings. Okay?"

Dani felt anger well up in herself now. She liked Dr. Robin a lot, but she didn't need a doctor.

"No, Dad. I can't explain what's happening, but I know what I saw. I didn't move that stained glass window."

He ran his fingers through his hair. "Dani, come sit here." He motioned for her to sit by him on the couch. He sat hugging her until she felt calm enough to go up to bed.

"I'm leaving your light on and the door open. I'm just a few feet away, honey. Call me if you need me." He kissed her good night and pulled the covers up tight. "You keep an eye out for my girl, okay, Riley?" Riley turned around in a circle then lay down beside Dani.

"Come on, boy." She snuggled Riley next to her.

She fell into a deep sleep but was awakened by a loud noise coming from downstairs. A crash of glass coupled with a ghoulish laugh reverberated through the house. Her dad rushed into her bedroom.

What's going on?" Dani thought his look changed when he realized she and Riley were in bed and the ungodly clatter came from the living room. "Wait here. Both of you."

He shut Dani's door, but she and Riley were up and out of bed. They followed him out and down the stairs. The moon illuminated the living room. Dani could see the closet door in the den where the stained glass window was housed. It was ajar, sparkling, and crystal had shattered everywhere on the floor.

"I thought I told you two to stay put. I don't want you to get hurt. Well, this explains the noise." Her dad had turned on a light and picked up the still-moving gargoyle. "The sensor was on, and the trees swaying in the moonlight set it off." He looked in the direction of the den and proceeded to the open closet. Bending down, he surveyed the shards of glass. "Keep Riley away from here." He exhaled, shook his head, and went to the kitchen. Riley took this opportunity to snarl at the closet.

"Go back to my room, Riley." Dani tugged at his collar and pointed him in the direction of her bedroom. She didn't want him to get cut on glass. He bounded back, and she pulled her door shut.

Returning with a dustpan, broom, and trash can, her dad paused and then proceeded to clean up.

Trembling and tearful, she sobbed, "Dad, you have to believe me. I don't know what's happening ..."

"Dani, I *do* believe you don't know what's happening. Let me clean this up and then we'll try to sort it out. You sit here." He hugged her and walked her to the sofa.

She watched as he picked up the bigger pieces of the broken glass and placed them in the trash.

"This was your mom's favorite cake pedestal, handed down to her from her great-aunt Martha." He wiped his eye, which made Dani burst into tears.

"Aw, don't cry." Placing the last piece in the trash, he moved to hug her. She ran to her room.

I'm so scared. Am I crazy? Why am I seeing and hearing these things? Why? She cried herself to sleep.

⸻

A strange tinkling sound and Riley's whimpering woke Dani. "What's wrong, Ri?" The golden retriever stood up, pointing at the window and moaning.

"It's nothing, boy, just a branch scratching the window." The giant pin oaks branches were clawing the window like bony fingers. A soft chiming bell-like sound startled Dani, forcing her to pull her sheets tight.

"What was that? You heard it too, didn't you?"

Riley wagged his tail, giving a low guttural sound.

Dani called him to her in the bed. Shaking, she hugged him close. A flood of moonlight cast a shadow on her wall of a weed-covered tombstone marking a grave. In the next instant, the image of the stained glass window appeared on her wall.

"Dad, Dad, Dad!" Dani screamed out, all the while clutching Riley to her.

"Unlock this door!" Her father was yelling, turning the handle and pounding, trying to get to her. "Dani, please!"

Dani was frozen in place, screaming and crying. In another instant, her dad opened the door.

"My God, Dani, what's going on? Why did you lock your door? You never lock it."

"I d-d-didn't." Dani could hardly get the words out.

"You couldn't have opened the door for me, could you? You're still in bed. Maybe it wasn't locked. Maybe I was trying too hard to get in and I jammed it or something."

"There was a grave with a tombstone and a shadow with lots of colors on my wall." She sputtered the words, her eyes wet with tears. She was shaking all over and not sure if the colors really were the stained glass or if she dreamed it.

"Okay, sweetheart, you had a bad nightmare. Snuggle under and I'll stay here until you calm down and fall asleep. It was just a bad dream—that's all."

Even while her dad was saying the words, Dani was not convinced. She knew it wasn't a nightmare. She planned to call Madisen in the morning and do some research on the Ouija board and the stained glass window. She was determined to find answers.

CHAPTER 4

Spirits and Snakes

stream of sunlight woke Dani. Groggy from sleep, she kicked her covers and then tensed. Her feet touched a huge lump at the bottom of the bed. The mound of covers rose in the air. Short guttural sounds emanated from it. The giant pyramid of quilt ascended and fell to the bed. A sniffing snout appeared.

"Oh my God, Riley, you scared me to death." Dani reached out and tousled his golden head, laughing with relief. He nuzzled her face. Grabbing her cell, she texted Madisen.

Dani: Hey

Madisen: Hey. I'm cleaning out my closet. Going for school clothes soon.

Dani: My dad's searching for a place to rent. I need to see you. I have more to tell you. Can you go for a hike in the park today?

Madisen: Probably. I'll ask. My mom can probably drop us off. Pick you up at noon at your house unless things change.

Dani: K

Dani smelled coffee and toast from the kitchen. She got out of bed and padded down the stairs.

"Morning, sleepyhead. How are we feeling today?" Her dad smiled, clearly trying to sound chipper, but Dani thought it sounded forced.

"Fine, I guess. Maybe." She moved toward him and hugged him.

"Maybe some breakfast will make you feel better. Omelet? Yogurt? Blueberries?"

Dani's stomach was growling, but she didn't feel like eating. Giving him a weak smile, she said, "Maybe a banana."

"I'm considering hitting the auction today. Want to come? You always loved the auction. I have a few things I'd like to leave with Brett. Maybe pick up a few bucks."

Dani stared at him. *God, that's the last place I want to go. And Dad hasn't been there since ...*

"Uh, I was going to ride bikes and hike with Madisen, if it's okay. Her mom can drive us to the park. The auction has sort of lost its appeal, ya know?"

"I do, honey. I need some cash, and I think I can get a good amount for a couple of paintings I have. I'm not planning to stay." Her dad looked down, making her sorry she had been so abrupt.

"Dani, should we talk about last night?"

"You were probably right, Dad. It was a dream—a scary one but *just* a dream."

"I'm here if you want to discuss anything. If you want to talk to someone else, besides our family doctor, I'm sure Dr. Robin would know a good therapist."

"I'll think about it, Dad." *I'm going to do more research on the supernatural first.*

"I have an appointment this afternoon. An interview. Possible job opportunity. A private party is interested in remodeling, more of a long-term renovation. Sounds promising. Then I'll be home and we'll get dinner. Pizza?"

"Sure. Half pepperoni, half mushroom, and double cheese?"

Dad smiled. "Um, sure."

Madisen's mom dropped them at the park. They rode their bikes for a few hours and then decided to hike along the creek.

"What do you think?" Dani asked, after relating the events of the evening before.

"I don't know, Dani. This is not good. One of those incidents by itself is frightening but altogether ... What are you going to do?"

"I don't know."

"Maybe your dad's right. You *have* been through a lot this year. Maybe you should talk about it with a counselor or something."

"I guess. I can't believe I didn't see and hear all those things."

"I'm your best friend. No matter what, I'm always here for you." Madisen hugged her and they continued.

Farther along the creek, a path appeared, taking them farther into the woods.

"I don't want to go in there. It's dark," Madisen said.

"Oh, come on. It's beautiful in the woods. Maybe we'll find a box turtle. You know how much you love turtles."

"Are you serious? I saw one on our road one time when I was walking with my mom. I was three. Haven't seen one since. I would love to find one. Okay, I'll go, but we'd better not see any snakes."

"This is a long and windy path. I wonder where it goes."

In front of them loomed a small stone house covered with weed and vines.

"Looks like one of those old houses used for cold storage." *Springhouses.* Dani remembered reading about them in social studies. "People stored their food in the creek to keep it cold. I think they were located on big estates.

Madisen was listening to Dani go on and on about springhouses—until she wasn't. "Dani, Dani?" she called.

Meanwhile, a distinct chill enveloped the still air. Dani encircled her arms around herself. A wave of thick, dense fog was headed right for her. Whispers and angry voices were coming from the springhouse. Something compelled her to move toward it.

Dani couldn't get her words out. She was as grounded as a stone statue. Unable to move, she saw a huge snake headed straight for her. Then it took on the human form of an old man with steel-gray eyes. He reached out as if to touch her, but he didn't.

"Oh, what happened? Where am I?" Rubbing her head, Dani tried to sit up.

Madisen was bending down to help her. "You tell me what happened. One minute you're behind me and then the next minute I find you here on the ground. You have a huge bump on your head. You need ice. I called my mom right before you came to. I'm worried about you, Dani. You could have a concussion."

"There was this icy cold in the air, and I saw the door to the springhouse open." Dani hadn't even gotten to the strange filmy form of the old ghoulish-looking man when Madisen stopped her.

"There wasn't any ice-cold anything. It's about eighty degrees out here. Besides, look at that springhouse. Nobody could get in there. It's covered with vines, probably poison ivy, and that wooden door is way too heavy to push open. I don't know what happened, Dani, but you need help, both physically and mentally."

Dani was in shock for real now. How could Madisen profess to be her friend one minute and then talk to her like this in the same day?

"Come on. Lean on me. My mom is meeting us at the road."

Dani allowed herself to be supported by Madisen, but they walked in silence.

Madisen is right. I'm in severe pain, both my head and my heart. And she caused half of it.

CHAPTER 5

Ghoul Haunting

ani's dad was in the kitchen when Madisen and her mom helped Dani from the car and walked her inside the house. His face wrinkled in concern. "What happened?"

"I'm not really sure, Ray," Madisen's mom said. "Somehow, Dani has a major lump on her head. The girls have been rather tight-lipped about it."

Dani wasn't sure how to take Madisen's mom's comments to her dad. She seemed amused rather than concerned. But her mom was an unusual person whom Dani never really got to know. They usually spent time at Dani's house, not Madisen's.

"Thank you." Dani heard her dad then say goodbye. Madisen hadn't said a single word to her since the incident in the woods.

"All right, young lady, get this ice on that lump. Let me see your eyes." Her dad surveyed her.

Checking for God knows what, Dani thought.

"We'll get some dinner into you, and then you'll tell me exactly where you were and what happened." He went to the kitchen after ordering her to sit up, not fall asleep, and keep ice on her head.

"What am I going to tell him, Ri? He'll flip if I tell him what I saw—what I *think* I saw."

Riley moaned and rested his head on his paws.

Dad brought her a cup of soup and some lemon water. The pizza they planned was abandoned in favor of lighter food in case of a concussion.

"Riley, you can head to the kitchen. Come on." She heard her dad feeding Riley, and then he returned with a sandwich for himself.

"I'm going to eat with you and listen to your story, Dani." He sat down with his sandwich and began munching, waiting for her to reply. "Nothing? All right, I'll start. Had fun at the auction. Sold my stuff at good prices, and then I bid on a Leith-Ross."

"What? You did?" Dani was taken aback.

"Just had a good time bidding it up. It was a beautiful winter scene depicting a creek in winter."

Dani felt nauseated just being reminded of the creek and the icy air earlier that day. "I'm glad you're going to auctions again, Dad."

"Me too, Dani. Just amused myself a little, not seriously. I know I can't afford a Leith-Ross."

She was about to confide in him when they were interrupted by the phone. While he was talking, she reconsidered and decided not to share what really happened. *He has a lot on his mind. I don't want to burden him until I know more.*

"That was the phone call I've been hoping would come," he said after he ended the call. "I have a renovation project that will take upwards of a year. I'll be the chief development head. I can start immediately."

"That's great, Dad!" Dani hugged him, happy for this long overdue piece of good news.

"Maybe our luck's changing, eh, girl? Now how did you get that lump?"

"Oh, I fell off my bike. A squirrel on the sidewalk startled me. It was stupid, and I was embarrassed to tell." Dani hoped she sounded convincing.

"Honey, you don't need to be ashamed. It was an accident. I'm concerned about your head."

For another few minutes, her dad grilled her about the lump and how her head felt. Then, satisfied that the bump was receding, he filled her in on the events leading up to his interview and the job he would be undertaking.

"You should start readying for bed. You have a special class meeting tomorrow morning at the middle school."

Dani had totally forgotten about that. She and Madisen had planned to go together. But now ...

"Uh, Dad, can you drop me off?"

"I thought you were going with Madisen."

"Uh, yeah, something came up. She's going to be late, so I said I'd go and meet her later."

Dani hated lying, but she seemed to be doing it a lot now. She passed the rest of the night without any noises or weird encounters and then found herself in front of the auditorium the next morning. Student volunteers directed the gathering inside to their seats.

"Welcome, students. We're sure you're looking forward to seeing the new gym and all the new additions and renovations."

A panel of teachers, counselors, and administrators introduced themselves, talked for an hour, and then assigned students to tour groups. She and Madisen ended up in the same small group.

"I'm sorry I said those things, Dani. I'm just worried about you."

"Don't be. I can take care of myself." Dani knew she was being hateful, but she was still hurt and angry at Madisen. She moved away from her.

"And this is the gym area." They turned a corner, and the guide took them into the gym. Dani looked and then fainted.

The group gathered around her. The guide spoke into his cell. Dani woke up in the nurse's suite with Madisen by her side.

"Where am I?"

"The nurse called your dad, but she couldn't reach him. My mom is coming to get us. You fainted when we came into the gym."

"The man—the same old horrible-looking man that I saw in the woods—was in the gym staring at me. He was trying to tell me something."

Dani started to cry, and Madisen sat next to her and put her arms around her. "I'm sorry I hurt you the other day, Dani. I was wrong. I want to be here for you." Dani couldn't help shaking and blubbering as she hugged Madisen. "I'll be here. We'll find out what's going on." Madisen squeezed her.

Madisen's mom took Dani home. Dad was in the kitchen. "Hey there. I was waiting for you to call so I could pick you up. But thanks for bring ..." He stopped in midsentence.

"The school nurse tried for an hour to call you, Dad. Finally, Madisen called her mom. Why didn't you answer?" she whined, tearing up.

"Dani, my phone didn't ring all day. I was here every second." He showed her his cell. There were no calls.

Dani shivered, still whimpering. Her dad held her and thanked Madisen and her mom. Her mom said that the nurse suggested a physical and that Dani had fainted on the tour. Dani was happy that Madisen never got to tell him about the strange apparition.

"We need to call Dr. Robin and have that lump you got the other day checked out. You might have a concussion. You stay here on the couch and rest until dinner."

Riley snuggled himself on the floor next to the couch, balanced his head on his paws, and sighed.

Dani fixed her head on the pillow and glanced into the dining room. Candles, the good china, Waterford Crystal, and cloth napkins graced the table. And three place settings? "Dad," she murmured with all the strength she could muster.

He came to the couch, cell in hand. "One second. I'm making an appointment for you. See if I can get one tonight. Thank God they have evening hours."

Returning in an apron, he brought some lemon water. "What do you need, honey?"

"Why are there three place settings? And why the good stuff?"

"I have some good news and bad news. I was going to tell you the bad later but ..."

Dani felt her stomach twinge. She wasn't in the mood for news, good or bad.

"My client or my boss, whichever, is coming for dinner. You'll love her."

"Her, *her*?" Dani bolted upright. Riley did as well.

"Now calm down. Her name is Mrs. Monaghan. She's a widower and seventy-six years old. She's just as sweet and lovely as can be, and she's hired me to renovate her home."

"What's the bad news?"

"Oh, I found a rental for us, but not in CB West. I'm afraid you won't be going to the same middle school."

Dani couldn't even concentrate on the rest of her Dad's

information. She was devastated that she would have to be in a new school. A new house was bad enough.

Dad was swirling a wooden spoon in the air, blathering about Mrs. Monaghan and his upcoming project.

The doorbell rang, and Dani felt like vomiting.

CHAPTER 6

A Mysterious Offer

"Mrs. Monaghan, please come in." Dani listened from the couch while her dad used his most charming voice.

"Thank you, Ray," a soft, sweet voice responded.

Riley had been hopping and swishing around, greeting the visitor at the door.

"Meet Riley."

"He's charming. I love dogs." Riley sniffed and sighed endearingly.

"This is my daughter, Dani. I'm afraid she had a little mishap on her bike; we may be looking at a concussion. I'm trying to call our doctor for an appointment. She didn't have any symptoms of a concussion, but she might now."

Dani listened to her dad rattling on. He was talking so fast. *Either this woman makes him nervous or he is really concerned now about my lump.*

"Dani, this is Mrs. Monaghan."

"Don't sit up, dear. I'm so sorry to hear that. And please, Ray, call me Irene." She reached out to pat Dani's shoulder and then gave her a warm, strong handshake.

Her eyes were beautiful green, the same color as Dani's mother's eyes. She wore gray pants and a simple Fair Isle pale green sweater with a beautiful jade oval on a gold chain. Her pure white hair encircled and brightened her face when she smiled. Dani's reaction when Irene touched her shoulder was instant suspicion. It was the oddest feeling she had ever experienced, both intensely calm and wary at the same time. She didn't want to be a part of Dad's new business venture, and she resented that he even invited this person to their home and was making a big deal of it. But Irene *was* the kind of older woman that you like immediately. It was the way she sat next to Dani and talked softly. *Maybe I just don't want a woman in our house. But she's so old that Dad wouldn't be interested.*

"May I offer you some liquid refreshment?"

What a goober. Just ask her if she wants wine.

"I would, thank you."

Dani listened to the pleasantries between them, noticing Irene readily accepting the glass of white wine. She stared at her from her vantage point on the couch, sizing her up. Her dad raised his glass. Irene followed suit.

"To a brighter future." They clinked glasses and drank.

"I have a baked brie with peach conserve and chopped walnuts. I hope you like it."

Dani watched and listened, analyzing every word. *He seems to be sucking up.*

The timer pinged in the kitchen, taking him away.

Hmm, I'm not sure what to make of Irene. She seems harmless, but there's something about her. I can't understand what I'm feeling. What's she doing? Inspecting the china?

Irene had carefully turned over a small bread and butter plate and then looked at the Waterford Crystal.

Hmm, apparently checking for the logo. Why would she care?

Dad returned with platters of food. Dani sat up and accompanied them to the dining room. Riley took up a place under the table, next to Dad, where he was sure to get table scraps.

"Thank you for inviting me to dinner. I always think it's easier to get to know a person in a relaxed atmosphere." She smiled at both of them, her green eyes twinkling.

You don't need to get to know me. Dani fake smiled.

"This looks delicious." Irene selected a piece of chicken covered with mushrooms and white wine sauce.

"I enjoy cooking, Irene."

"I do as well. Perhaps you'll both come and I'll cook for you."

Dani listened throughout dinner, responding with one-word monotone replies. They covered every subject known to man.

"I never had children, although my husband and I wanted a houseful. Unfortunately, it wasn't to be."

"I'm so sorry."

"Thank you. So then we decided to restore the mansion and then foster teenagers."

Dani's jaw dropped. *Are you kidding me?* "I never met anyone who actually *wanted* teenagers," she voiced.

Irene smiled at her. Ray ignored Dani's remark and glared at her.

What? What's wrong with that comment?

"Irene, how long have you lived there?" Dad continued staring at Dani while addressing Irene.

"A few weeks. My distant cousin, whom I never met, inherited the estate. He never lived there, possibly because he couldn't afford the repairs. He passed away and left it to me. My husband and I restored the roof and did major structural repairs. We were getting ready to move in and get to the actual decor when he became ill and passed suddenly. I abandoned our plans. I had no desire to continue until recently."

"What happened recently?" Dani was quick to catch that one. But Irene's mood clearly dimmed, and she claimed that it was time.

What did that mean? She's hiding the real reason. "Um, you didn't say why you want to renovate now," Dani probed.

"No, I didn't, dear." Her green eyes stared straight at Dani.

Ooh, definitely awkward.

"It's a big mansion and a lonely place. It needs a total makeover. Bright colors and fabrics. New furniture. I'm excited for you both to see it."

Dani blinked. *Why would I want to see it? It's Dad's job.*

As if reading her mind, Irene looked right at Dani. "I'm toying with an idea. Suppose you two come and look around. I understand you've sold this place and you'll be in need of a new home. There's plenty of room in the manor. I'd love for you to live with me while you renovate it."

What? We went from dinner with you to moving in? Who does that?

"You want us to live with you? We can't. We don't even know you." Dani's voice grew louder with every syllable.

"Watch it, young lady. You're out of line." Her dad's voice was harsh.

Irene laid her hand on his to quiet him. "Dani, I know this is all very new. I appreciate what you must be feeling. I've presented my idea, and now I'm going to give you time to digest it. In the meantime, I'd like you to come stay overnight and familiarize yourselves."

She certainly is adamant that we visit and accept her proposal.

"I think it's a wonderful idea, Irene, and I will look forward to visiting. I'm sure Dani will too after she gives it some thought. I could check out what the job will entail while we're there."

Are you crazy? Yeah, your job, not mine. Dani scowled at him. "What about Riley?" Dani demanded.

"He's very welcome too, my dear. We'll have a splendid visit. I'll take you on a tour of all the gardens as well."

Her sullen mood changed quickly. As soon as she thought my dad was willing to consider the prospect, she was beaming. Can she be trusted? I don't have a good feeling about her.

"And, Dani, the mansion is within your middle school district. You won't have to change schools."

Dani's stomach tightened. "How do you know where my middle school is, Irene?"

"We have the same zip, dear." Irene laughed.

Dinner ended on a positive note, and Dad and Irene were left to set up a date for the visit.

Dani called Madisen as soon as she could. "Can you stay overnight tomorrow? I need to see you, and I want to tell you all about Irene."

"Irene who?"

"Exactly. All of a sudden, this woman is in our lives. I can't explain what's going on. I have mixed feelings about her."

"Why? Do you think your dad's interested in her?"

"Like *dating* interested? No. She's, like, a hundred years old. I just have a weird sense when I'm around her, like there's something mysterious about her. I can't explain it."

They finished their conversation, planning to spend the next day and night together.

Dad was happy that Madisen was there because he was gathering information about restoring old mansions and was out late.

"Okay, let's go to my room and finish reading about that Ouija board."

"What? Why? What does this have to do with anything about Irene?"

"I don't know. But the board somehow got to my room. We need to finish reading the rules and ask it some questions."

"Well, okay, as long as you realize it's just a game." Madisen twisted her hair when she said this.

"Yeah, right." Dani didn't know where her courage was coming from but she was hot on the pursuit of answers.

After going over the rules, they set the board up and lit some candles. Riley was penned in the kitchen for safety.

"The rules say not to use this in your own house. So what are we doing?"

"Well, technically we're going to be moving soon so it won't be our house."

"And," Madisen went on, "you shouldn't ask about other people."

"I'll start," Dani said, ignoring her.

"Is Irene really who she says she is?" Dani's hands were set on the planchette as it moved to the capital letter *N*. Then it spelled out *no*.

"Oh, cool. I knew it."

The planchette spun around the board, drawing a figure eight.

"OMG!" Madisen gasped. "It's an evil spirit. We contacted an evil spirit."

"Are you a bad spirit?" Dani asked.

No.

"Who are you?"

The planchette moved to the letter *N*. Then the candles blew out. The girls screamed, and the board flew across Dani's room. Madisen jumped for the lights. Riley was barking downstairs.

"That thing is dangerous, Dani." They stood, hugging each other. "What do you suppose that meant?" Madisen whispered.

"I d-don't know, but I don't want to mess with that board anymore," Dani stuttered.

"Let's put it back in the basement. This time I'm putting that planchette in separately."

They carted the box to the basement and secured it in a cabinet. "I'd like to do one more thing," Dani said.

"It better not involve summoning spirits," Madisen whined.

"I want to do some research on the mansion off of Green Street. Irene said a tragedy happened there but she never even checked into it. If that were left to me by my ancestors with all that history about it, I would want to know what was what."

Dani Googled the property but could only guess at the location. A story did come up about a murder of a young family, heir to the shipbuilding industry in Philadelphia and a mentally ill twin.

"I don't have a name or address, so I really can't tell anything from this. I need to find out more from Irene without her knowing why I want to know."

"Why do you want to know?"

"She's invited us to visit the place."

CHAPTER 7

A Bronze Bulldog

She listened, arms crossed, while her dad outlined his plan for the near future. He turned off the country road and drove through black wrought iron gates—supported on either side by a colossal stone fence—and onto a long gravel drive.

"Look at these giant pin oaks. They're magnificent. And the boxwoods. Put the window down so you can smell them."

"Right." Dani obliged and hit the window button.

Massive graying columns loomed in front of them, bracing up the crumbling portico of what looked like a once-stately manor.

"How old is this place?"

"I think Irene said it was built in the early eighteen hundreds." Her dad sniffed the air. "Man, this is what I call living. Smell the air?"

"We should never have agreed to stay overnight. The place looks creepy."

"Dani, that's why I've been hired—to un-creep it." Her dad laughed. "This will give me a better feel for the place. I can't wait to see inside."

Right. Looks like ghosts are ready to appear at any moment.

"Some of those windows on the second floor are boarded up." Dani wrapped her arms around herself.

"Irene said it needed renovations, especially the east wing. It's not in use right now. Look at that cool statue." Her dad parked the car in the semicircle of boxwood flanking the circular drive in front and pointed to a life-size stone statue of a bulldog.

Dani saw it as she touched the door handle and fell from the car. Riley bounded out and ran to the statue, jumping and barking around it.

"Dani, be careful. What are you doing?" Dad ran to her side of the car and helped her up.

The bulldog. She twirled her hair, drawing closer to her dad.

"It's great!" He kept his arm around her and walked her up the wide marble stairs, where the statue sat gracing the entry.

Riley gave a resounding howl and backed away from it.

"Is something wrong, honey?"

"It resembles the bulldog that Riley and I saw."

"Dani, really? That could have been any dog. Honey, that looks to be a very expensive and old bronze statue. It has nothing to do with your sighting, I'm sure."

He doesn't sound sure. He sounds worried. She was about to protest staying the night when the massive double doors opened.

"Good morning, everyone. I'm delighted to see you." Irene's green eyes twinkled as she smiled. "Please come in."

Riley bounded right through the doors, sniffing and growling the entire time.

"Riley, settle. He's usually pretty docile, Irene. Must be a new place and all."

Yeah, right. There's something eerie about this place. I feel it too. Dani stayed close to her dad, knowing that he wouldn't be happy if she didn't act normal, but she wasn't willing to stray from him.

The door creaked behind them as Irene moved to close it. Dani shivered as the noise reverberated up the massive staircase.

"This place is incredible, Irene. I can understand you wanting to restore it." Her dad rubbed his hands through his hair, holding onto his Phillies cap.

Dani's eye followed the path of the center hall stairs up to a wall of angled bay windows that rose at the top of the stairs.

"These rooms exuded grandeur at one time." Irene expressed her enthusiasm by spreading her hands and pointing. "Follow me into the ballroom. The fading wallpaper and cracking plaster portray a sign of richer days."

As they trailed behind her, Dani's eye went up to the landing on the stairway. She thought she caught a glimpse of a white filmy movement. She did a double take. A flowery scent filled the air but she didn't see any around her.

Irene probably has an air freshener stashed somewhere.

Riley continued his guttural moans.

Something's wrong. He never growls. She scooted closer to her dad.

"Beautiful chandelier, Irene. They don't make them like that anymore."

"Thank you. I did research *some* things. I found that the architecture, banisters, stairwells, and lighting designs were created by Richard Morris Hunt, the same man who created the Breakers and the Biltmore."

"Is that right? I can envision ladies in magnificent gowns waltzing around this room."

He's mesmerized by all this.

The dark green velvet drapes swayed like a wave on the sea. Irene smiled at Dani. "I'm afraid this room can be quite drafty. The windows need replacing, and the high ceilings don't support warm and cozy. Let's move to the library and I'll get us some refreshments. I spend most of my time in the library because it's so snug."

They followed Irene out of the ballroom to a small alcove behind the massive main staircase.

Dad just keeps chirping like a bird about every archaic piece of art or furniture he sees. He really is happy around Irene.

"There. You relax in here and I'll get my homemade sticky buns and hot chocolate from the kitchen." Irene opened the door into a pale blue room with a welcoming fireplace.

"Let me help you, Irene."

Dani started to object. "Dad, no ..."

Her dad's tense smile indicated that she should stay there. "I'll help Irene."

Great. Leave me alone here in this seriously sinister excuse for a house. "Fine, Dad."

Dani hugged Riley to her and sat on the sofa, which was remarkably new, surveying the room. "I've never been in a house that had its own library, Ri." Dani surprised herself by being interested.

Wood-paneled shelves stretching from floor to ceiling and holding a massive collection of books stone surrounded the stone. A carved wooden desk graced the other side of the room, next to a tall window.

Riley sighed. A warm, secure feeling engulfed Dani. "This room *is* nice. I like being in here." Riley sighed again, and Dani walked closer to the fireplace.

Irene and Dad returned with a huge plate of homemade cinnamon buns and hot chocolate.

"Are you both ready to hear more of what I do know about the property?" Irene gave them each a paper napkin with an old-fashioned fall flower design and a pastry while Dad poured the chocolate, nodding with a huge grin at Irene.

"The design and construction were begun in eighteen seventy-nine. The owner, a young married merchant, returned from England with his Irish bride. They engaged a well-known architect, also a personal friend, to overseer the project. I'm afraid that's all I know. The rest is rumor and conjecture passed down to me through my mother's ancestors."

Dani munched on her snack and listened. She sensed a familiarity with this room and the facts that Irene related. *But how?* "What rumors, Irene?" Dani was curious now.

"Oh, my dear, there are rumors of the tragic deaths of the original owners, but I don't know any more than that."

Yikes, deaths here? Really?

"There are five bedrooms with adjoining baths on the second floor. I'm afraid only three are in livable condition. I've chosen the two in the west wing for you and Dani, and I'll be in the one in the east wing."

Eating her snack, still feeling warm and secure, Dani found herself as mesmerized as her dad. Irene's sweet voice made for great storytelling as she continued relating facts about the old mansion.

"My dear husband and I were working on the first-floor rooms when he became ill. There are six rooms altogether down here. Only the library has been totally redone to my satisfaction. Are we ready to take a tour?"

"Yes." Dani rose from the couch first and headed toward the door.

"I'm glad you're so anxious, young lady." Her dad winked at Irene.

"Perhaps we just needed some food and a warm fire." Irene smiled back.

No, I want to see this whole place. The mansion is welcoming me. I feel it. Dani was definitely feeling more upbeat, but she couldn't explain the change.

"What's down this way, Irene?" Dani proceeded down the hall to the right.

"You're headed to the main dining hall, the kitchen, and

the pantry, dear. Take a right at that door." Laughing, Irene and Dani's dad rushed to catch up to Dani and Riley.

"This is gigantic." Dani moved through the tall double wooden doors.

"Gorgeous. These are mahogany aren't they?" her dad asked.

"Yes, and Gothic style."

"They look like church doors." Dani put her hand out, smoothing it over the panel.

"Wait until we get to the chapel if you want to see Gothic church doors." Irene led them into the dining room.

"The chapel?" Dani and her dad answered in unison.

"That is, the part that is *left* of the chapel. The structure is gone, destroyed by fire. Just the stone footprint remains, in addition to the entry doors, ironically. I don't have any information other than that. I wish I did."

"Why is that ironic, Irene?"

"The doors are carved hardwood, but everything else burned to the ground, leaving no trace. It's as if the doors stood to a testament of something."

Dani shuddered and hugged herself, the eerie feeling returning.

Irene chattered on as she led them through the kitchen, the butler's pantry, and then out to the arboretum. "This must have been truly wonderful in its day, Ray. Notice these bay windows. In fact, all the windows in this house are different. Mr. Hunt, the architect, designed them that way, and the owner must have agreed."

"Where's the chapel, Irene?" Dani interrupted. She could see that they had come to the end of the house.

"It used to be through that french door. That's all that remains."

Dani moved toward the glass doors and went outside. *That*

was *the foundation of the chapel.* Irene and her dad followed. Riley sniffed, whimpered, and uttered a shrill bark.

"Ri, come here, boy. There could be nails or glass in there." Dad reached for his collar.

Beautiful tall arched doors, housed on either side by stone, led into a partially remaining burned-out stone structure.

An eerie whisper filled the air. "Unlock the secret. Unlock the secret."

CHAPTER 8

Weird Whispers Again

Dani jumped. "What?" She turned to Irene and her dad. "What did you say?"

"We haven't said anything, Dani." Her dad raised his hands palms up.

"I heard a whisper."

"Probably the wind, dear. It is a bit chilly. Let's get back inside and I'll show you the second floor." Irene and Riley led the way. Her dad took Dani's arm.

"I'm right here, sweetheart. No worries." He squeezed her arm and then moved them forward.

Dani turned around and surveyed the ruins of the chapel. *I know what I heard. What secret?*

They caught up to Irene as she was leading the way up the center hall staircase. Stopping on the second-floor landing, Dani's nose was assailed again by the rich scent of lavender flowers.

"Irene, what air freshener do you buy? I've never smelled a lavender one that nice."

"Oh, my dear, I don't have anything. I don't smell lavender, of course. My nose isn't what it used to be." She looked at Dani with an "I'm sorry to disappoint" smile. "Come, I'll show you the rooms where you will be sleeping."

Carrying their overnight bags, Dani, Riley, and Dad trudged behind Irene.

"This will be your room, Dani. I hope you like it, dear. I didn't know what colors or things you would like in a room, so I went on my first impression of you. I had it done earlier this week."

Entering the room with the tallest ceilings and windows Dani had ever seen, she lost her breath. She ran over to the window seats, smoothing her hands along the pale green striped cushions. Then she climbed up to survey the beautiful lawn beneath her room.

"It's gorgeous, Irene. I love green, and I love the flowery drapes, and the desk, and the bureau and the bed, and everything."

"Oh, my dear, I'm delighted that you like it. And this will be your own bathroom. Each bedroom has its own bathroom. Quite a luxury for the eighteen hundreds."

Dani welled up in tears when she saw the bathroom. Lavender flowered hand towels and bath towels hung on brass bars. The room was a delicate shade of lavender paint, and lavender soap sat daintily on a porcelain dish.

"My mom loved lavender. We haven't had any purple flowers or towels or anything since she …"

"There, there, dear. I didn't want you to be sad." Irene hugged her.

"I'm not. I'm very happy and very grateful to you for this beautiful room."

"You may bring your own comforter and things or we can purchase a new one."

"I'm sure this will be wonderful. If we stay here, that is."

Ray shifted his feet. Dani realized that he was suddenly uncomfortable.

"I know you do your best, Dad, but I miss those things Mom did for us." He moved to embrace her. "Let's see more, Irene."

"I think we're overwhelmed by y-your generosity." Ray stammered. Dani knew what he was feeling.

The adjoining room was to be her dad's.

"I thought this would be good because it has a door leading right into your room. That way, you and Dani can be next to each other since it's quite a distance across these halls."

Dad's room was a pale blue with a new navy comforter and matching drapes. His bath had a claw-foot tub and adjoining shower. Dani stared at the tub. *Glad that thing isn't in my room. It's hideous.*

"This is a wonderful antique chest. Is it Chippendale?"

Is it Chippendale? Really, Dad? She had to smile. *He knows it's Chippendale.*

"It is, and it was already here, like so many other pieces that were here when we moved in. It was as if the inhabitants just up and left."

Climbing up the circular stairs to the third level, Dani gaped at the ceiling. A huge fresco of angels was painted above them.

"I'm afraid these rooms are now the least desirable in the mansion. But they were once lovely."

Dani and Riley tagged behind. A chill in the air forced her to hug her arms around herself, and she sensed another presence in the room. Turning, she didn't see anyone. She rushed to catch up.

"These rooms are empty, which makes them look bigger. The furniture that remains suggests that they were all guest bedrooms. You know, travel back then tended to take a couple of days by trap or carriage from Philadelphia or New York. People stayed for days or weeks and had marvelous balls and dinner parties. Perhaps we shall too someday, eh, Dani?"

Least desirable rooms is an understatement. Dani gazed at the room in front of her. Light bulbs hung by wires from the ceiling, walls were cracked, and the paint was gray. A thought she didn't want to have formed in her head; *haunted house* etched itself in her mind.

"I would love it if you two—and Riley, of course—would come here to live with me."

Riley smiled his doggy smile and let out a sigh.

"Since my husband passed, I haven't enjoyed my life."

I haven't enjoyed mine since my mom died, so we're even. And I'm not thrilled with this mansion since I've seen this floor. I feel bad for you, Irene, but yikes. I don't know about this mansion.

Riley scampered away and entered a room in the middle of the hall. Dani followed him. "Get back here, Riley. I don't want us to get separated." She gasped as she followed him into the room. A white shape fluttered into view. Laughing, her hands shook as she went to the open window, pulled the torn white curtain inside, and closed it. "Oh God, I thought that was a ghost." The room was icy, colder than it should have been for the weather outside.

Hearing the sound of muted voices from down the hall, she turned to leave. Riley growled and bared his teeth. "Stop, Riley. It's just Irene and Dad."

He ignored her, sniffing around the room, covering every corner, and snarling.

The door slammed closed.

"Oh, great." She grabbed the knob and turned it, but it appeared to be locked. She panicked a little and tried to be rational. *I'm sure it's just stuck.* She looked around the room for something she could use to open it. Her eyes were drawn to a mirror over a bureau.

Help.

Dani thought the word was written on the stained glass window, but when she looked again, it was gone. She turned back to the door, which now was ajar.

"Let's not panic, Riley." *My heart is pounding, and I'm shaking all over, but let's try to explain all this. I can't.* "Let's get out of here, Riley."

Upon entering the corridor, she could hear the voices from the left side of the hall; Irene and Dad were on the opposite side. Riley bolted toward them, leaving Dani frozen to her spot. *I'm hearing voices. I'm seeing things.*

CHAPTER 9

Face in Tower Window

"We didn't do a lot of research. The only information came from letters from my mother's cousins, and we don't know if they are accurate facts or pure gossip." She and Ray shared a laugh.

"Irene?" Dani moved in a minute to where they talked. "Do you have people working here in the house?"

"No, dear. I'm not hiring a single soul until your father and I concur." She continued. "I have a letter from my mother stating that a great tragedy occurred here, but I have no other information about it."

Dani froze. *Tragedy? What did that mean? Why didn't she want to know why I asked about people in the house? She told us people died here. How?* "Irene, aren't you curious about the history of this mansion? I would want to know what the tragedy was all about."

"Really, Dani? I guess I just never had time to pursue that."

Very unconvincing. "Where do those stairs go, Irene?"

"That's the tower room. I've never been up there. My husband said the doors lead to stairs and another door that is boarded up.

We were going to explore but never got the chance." She paused. "Look at the time. I've packed a picnic for us. We can eat it outside and then explore the gardens and woods."

Moments later, they found themselves on a bench of stone surrounded by a horseshoe-shaped stone table amid a cluster of giant boxwood. "These must be hundreds of years old," her dad said. I don't believe I've ever seen boxwood this tall. Except ..." He glanced at Dani.

Yes, I remember the stories Mom told about the boxwood. She loved the pungent smell, and it always reminded her of your honeymoon in England. She ignored his glance.

"You'll love the gardens, then. Eat up." She placed an array of fried chicken, salad, blueberry pie, and lemonade on a cloth of blue checks.

"Irene, there are so many niches to go in and out of, and ..." Dani stopped in midsentence. While she was pointing all around the property, her eye fell on the window up in the tower room. A face stared out at her. Then it was gone.

"Yes, dear? You were saying?"

"Um, just that it would be fun." *Irene, really? No servants or help working for you? It's such a big place not to have any help.* "I thought I saw a face in the window."

"No, dear. It's probably a reflection from the sun. I hope your father will help me decide what we need and who to engage." Irene was clearly dismissing the mention of a face.

Dani pondered the morning. *Weird. Irene gets tons of points for her food, but that third floor ... those voices. And now the face in the tower room. She's hiding something.*

The sound of Irene's voice brought Dani back to the conversation. "There's a pond and a pool that's at least a century old, gardens, and woods—about a twenty-acre package altogether— oh, and a charming old stone springhouse."

Dani looked up. "Springhouse?" *I wonder what that looks like. Couldn't be the same one Madisen and I found. Or could it? We were somewhere near here.*

"I don't have a gardener, so the gardens are in need of trimming and weeding, but you can see that they were once quite something in their day. Two of the twenty acres are formal; the rest are woods. This is the rose garden." They walked from their picnic to a white picket fenced-in area with many rose bushes, some still blooming. "It's my favorite, and I would love to spend time here in the spring. Do you like to garden, Dani?"

Spring? Did we even agree to live here? Does she even think we'll be here in the spring? "I don't know a lot about gardening. My mom did, and I helped sometimes."

Nausea engulfed her. Her emotions were vacillating between fear and loss. The scents of the varied color rose bushes, some withering and weed entangled, reminded Dani of her mother and working in her garden. She picked at a finger and tried not to cry.

"Dani, I hope I didn't say something to upset you." Irene reached a hand out to Dani's hand. Then her dad put his arm around her shoulder.

"This garden sort of reminded me of my mom and me gardening together."

"There, there, dear. I understand. This is a very emotional time for you."

"Let's see the rest, Irene. I'm okay now." Dani sniffled and blew her nose on a tissue that Irene provided from her pocket. They moved on.

"We have many varieties of trees, most over a hundred years old."

They walked what seemed like quite a distance, until they reached another set of wide marble stairs leading down into the woods.

"Let's explore the springhouse." Irene clapped her hands, chatting about how she and her husband discovered it on one of their walks along the creek bed.

Dani panicked. The area of woods they were entering had a host of white pine trees creating a grove deeper into the woods along a creek. The surrounding foliage was very similar to the location where she and Madisen had found *their* springhouse.

Dad wiped sweat from his forehead. "This is an extensive property, Irene."

"Yes, it is. There." Irene pointed ahead of her.

Dani looked in that direction. Stunned, she gasped.

CHAPTER 10

Nathan's Story

Autumn 1896

Nathan finished part of his sketch and began collecting his artists' accoutrements.

"Sir Bernie, here, boy." Whistling for his English bulldog, he spied him chasing down a butterfly.

"Have fun, Bernie. That's probably one of the last butterflies of the season." He looked around as he gathered his things, smiling at the rich fall colors of the beautiful Bucks County countryside. He looked at the pup, envying his freedom. "If only I could be a pup and be treated as well as you are." The burly brindle was approaching eight years, and he still romped like a puppy.

The impending late afternoon chill started to fill the air. The smoky scents of wood mingled with a rich stew of some sort from a nearby chimney made his stomach growl.

"I almost lost track of the time, Bernard. Mrs. Wythe will be home from market and preparing supper. She doesn't take lightly to latecomers. To keep her on our side, we have to do as she wishes." He winked at the dog and finished wrapping the pastels in the brown paper they came in, storing them in the tin he used to carry them.

"Let's keep them in the springhouse, Bernard. They've been safe there all summer." Bernard followed Nathan as he took his wooden easel, canvases, and pastel tin and secured them between stones in the wall of the little stone enclosure. His rested his hand on the stone for a moment, thinking about his da back in England. It was he, his mother's father, who knew his talent and passion for drawing, who sent the pastels. Da only visited once from England. His grandfather was a strong and huge man, having worked his way from Ireland to England as a dockworker.

"Da was a very resourceful man, Berns. I wish you could have known him. He bought one small ship and turned it into an empire. He was very wealthy. I deserve to have his wealth for art school and to support myself along with paintings. I am being treated poorly by Father."

The sun slid behind the manor, illuminating its many windows. Lights were beginning to shine in the first-floor rooms.

"Let's run, Bernard. If we're fast, we'll make it just in time to wash up."

Sprinting down the hill, laughing and barking, the young man and his dog approached the side of the manor. Mrs. Wythe's carriage was parked at the door.

"Sarah Wythe and old James have returned from market day. We can look forward to a sumptuous dinner. What's that in the drive, Bernard?"

A black carriage similar to his father's trap stood in front of the circular drive to the mansion. It was newer and shinier than his father's was. "Company, maybe?"

Being an only child and motherless, Nathan looked forward to visitors most of the time.

He continued to the kitchen wing of the manor, where Sarah Wythe greeted him. "Quickly, young Nathan. You're late. I hope you haven't been tromping away again in those woods." Her tone was agitated but guarded. Nathan thought she adored him because she gave him anything he wanted to make him happy. The concern in her voice could mean only one thing.

"Your father has come from the city for the night. He has a new trap and a new lady friend. They'll be here for dinner and leave in the morning. Please don't cause a fuss, dear."

Nathan tried to calm her with his humor. "I wasn't tromping around in the woods, dear Sarah." He winked and smiled at her. "I was sketching."

"You know what I'm telling you, boy. We'll all be in trouble."

"Nonsense. My lips are sealed." He gave her a hug, pulling her close. But she tensed up.

"Well, take Sir Bernie and feed him—then put him in your wing. You can let him out after dinner. He won't be welcome in the dining room. I put some extra beef scraps and carrots aside for him."

"We'll go wash up and be on our best behavior. Don't want to upset the *master*." He emphasized the word and saw Sarah attempt to smile.

"I've a wonderful pheasant dish and a special apple pie for you. I know they're your favorites. Now don't be long."

Trudging up the back staircase from the kitchen, Nathan headed to his bedroom and wing on the third floor. His father moved him there on his last birthday to provide him more space, but Nathan believed it was convenient for his father. He was away from the central area and had no access to the rest of the house. His room was accessed by one door from the kitchen.

He sighed. "I'm supposed to feel lucky, Bernard. I have this wonderful manor, a loving caretaker in Sarah, and this splendid

Bucks County countryside to sketch and paint. And you— how could I forget you?" He hugged the bulldog so tight that the animal whimpered. "Don't be a wimp, Bernard."

He thought about his father. An ominous cloud hung over the manor whenever his father was there. Nathan could feel it in Sarah's reserved manner and old James's speech and actions. Nathan just thought his father was reserved and cold, although he had experienced his temper. Were Sarah and old James afraid of him? If so, then why would they stay on? "I guess that's something to ponder, eh, Bernard?" The dog looked up and sighed.

"Yes, I know how you feel." Nathan smiled. "I'm going to the dining hall, but I'll bring you a treat later." Satisfied that he looked presentable, Nathan headed downstairs.

Laughter emanated from the ballroom, strange to his ears. Dinners with his father were usually dismal. A new voice must be the woman Sarah mentioned.

"Ah, there you are, Nathan." Nathan waited for a stern rebuke for his tardiness, but none came. He chose to appear pleasant.

"Good evening, Father. I'm surprised to see you here in the middle of the week." Smiling, he shook his father's hand. "But glad nonetheless."

The man winced at this reference to "Father." The man seated at the head of the table had graying brown hair, hazel eyes, and an expensive three-piece suit. His brow betrayed years of worry. "I have some business to attend to early tomorrow in the area, so I asked this charming lady to join me for dinner and enjoy the autumn countryside."

Nathan was not impressed. She giggled too much, laughed too loud, and couldn't carry on conversation during dinner. Her hair was blonde and wildly curly, as if to say she was carefree. She wore many diamonds, rings, bracelets, and necklaces. Her clothes looked expensive but were loud, unrefined colors.

"Tell me what Tutor taught you today."

"Um …" Nathan stuttered to respond, catching Sarah's eye as she replenished a platter.

"Tutor was not well today, so Nathan read his books and worked on future assignments, sir."

Thank God for you, Sarah. He shot her a knowing glance. She almost dropped the serving spoon.

Nathan smiled. "I did have time to read some literature. Tutor left a magazine article written by one Edgar Allen Poe. I found his references to murder quite intriguing." The woman giggled, but his father glared and downed his wine.

"I see. In the future, I would like to be informed of Tutor's illnesses."

"It's never happened before, sir. I'm sure it will not again." Sarah was quick to intervene with his father. She always protected the boy from any punishment if she could. Nathan was glad she didn't mention that he had spent the entire day sketching with Bernard in the woods.

When dinner ended, he was glad. "If you'll excuse me, it was lovely to meet you." He returned to his room thinking how he could tolerate the visits with his father as long as they were infrequent.

CHAPTER 11

Boy in the Album

Irene's voice sounded in her ear. "My goodness, Dani. What is it?"

"Uh, what?" Dani's hand covered her mouth.

"You saw something, right? You let out a shout. Perhaps we spent too much time outside in the heat."

"It's not that hot out here, Irene. Dani, do you feel sick?"

Her dad's worried whisper jolted her memory. *That springhouse. The stone building was covered with weeds and overgrown vines. It was the same one that Madisen and I encountered.*

"I'm fine, Dad. Maybe I should have had more water."

"Are you serious? You drank about a gallon between lunch and now." Her father kneeled next to her, his face wrinkled with worry. "I think we should return to the house. Maybe you've had too much walking."

She couldn't tell them it was the same springhouse she'd seen with Madisen. "Maybe you're right, Dad. I am a little tired."

But Irene continued toward the springhouse as if she hadn't heard a word. *What is she doing? I want to leave this place.*

"I'd like to see inside." Irene approached the stone edifice and tried the door. "Oh dear, it's locked tight. I don't have a clue where a key would be found."

Dani couldn't believe her ears. *Locked tight? It was wide open the other day. If Irene doesn't have a key, who does?*

"It functioned as cold storage for a carriage house that stood nearby. It was destroyed by fire in the eighteen nineties. The springhouse never served a purpose after that. Oh, the air is getting chilly. Yes, let's start back. Ray, you're right. Enough adventure for one day."

"Dani, are you sure you can walk back?"

I'm freezing. I can't wait to get out of here. "I'm good."

Starting up the trail that led out of the woods, Dani realized that Riley wasn't with them. "Riley? Here, boy." She turned to wait for him, and he bounded from behind some bushes and flew past her, heading up the group.

The snap of a branch forced her to look behind her. *The door is wide open.*

Dani couldn't be sure if these things were real or if she was imagining them. She only knew that she was jumpier than ever and on the verge of tears at every moment. She was happy when they reached the mansion at last.

"Why don't you two relax here in the library while I start preparing dinner?"

Dani yawned and sat on the couch. Riley joined her. "I'm really sleepy."

"Tell you what. I'll sit with you until you fall asleep, and then I'll help Irene in the kitchen."

"I can handle the dinner, Ray, but we could discuss your employment and details regarding the renovations. If that's okay with you and Dani." She raised her eyes at Dani for approval.

Nodding and yawning, Dani snuggled under the afghan and fell fast asleep.

A noise startled her awake. She was aware of the tinkling of bells. "It's dark. How long did I sleep, Riley?" Riley's jowls opened wide, exhaling a snort and then a sigh in response. "I see you slept too." Stretching, she got up and looked around.

"I love this library and the floor-to-ceiling shelves. There must be hundreds of book in here." Intrigued by the wide selection, she moved from shelf to shelf and perused the titles.

"What's this? Oh, a row of old photo albums. Let's see if there are any pictures of the previous owners, Riley." It was filled with sepia-colored pictures of the mansion. The gardens, with the roses in bloom, all in the same brownish tint, were well maintained.

"Look, Riley." She had turned a page to face a chunky bulldog. "He looks like the one we saw at the town house. Who's this boy next to him? We should ask Irene if she knows anything about them."

A voice from behind startled her. "Dani, are you feeling better?"

"Irene, you scared me. Yes, I'm much better. Thank you. I guess I needed to sleep. We were looking through these old albums. Do you know anything about this boy and bulldog?"

Irene's reaction was not what Dani expected. "No, I'm afraid I don't know anything. Dinner's ready if you'd like to come, dear." She extended an arm for Dani to lead the way toward the kitchen.

The subject of the boy and bulldog was dropped while Dani set the table and Irene and Dad placed platters and bowls of food on the table.

Irene proclaimed that she was happy to cook for people who enjoyed eating. Her mood had changed since the encounter in the library, but Dani's had too. The warm kitchen and wonderful food relaxed her.

I need to pursue this again. I'm sure she knows something. "Irene, I'd like to research the history of the people of this property. I know you would like to research the decor, but I think the people hold the real story."

"That may be a possibility." She kept cutting the meat, more than three people would need. "I wasn't close to my cousins, and they were the direct line of descendants, not my mother's family." She concentrated on her roast beef. "Y-yes, why of course we can research the history of the property." Her green eyes hesitated as she forced a smile at Dani.

My questions are making her edgy.

Dinner ended, and they cleaned up together, Irene proposing her plan for rehab, Dad countering with his ideas. They meshed well. Irene suggested a game of Harry Potter Clue, amazing Dani with her knowledge of the popular series. The chiming grandfather clock alerted them to the hour.

"I was having so much, Irene, that I lost track of the time." He checked his watch. "We should be heading for bed, right, Dani?"

Dani was now too excited and not tired, but what choice did she have? "I guess, Dad."

Irene motioned them to follow. "All that fresh air wore us out. I'll help you get settled in your rooms."

Once tucked in, Dani cuddled Riley. "Today was an odd day, Ri." He whined in agreement. Dani reached for her phone. "Let's see what we can uncover."

She searched the internet for old newspaper articles until she couldn't keep her eyes open.

―――

Frying bacon and fresh coffee smells awakened Dani. She sat up remembering where she was and noticed that Riley was missing. He was an expert at turning handles. The kitchen aromas must have gotten to him too. He would be there begging for scraps.

Thank God no events *during the night.*" She padded down the wide staircase. Stopping at the library door, she was about to enter when a hand tapped her shoulder.

"Oh, Irene, you startled me."

"I didn't mean to, dear. I have some breakfast ready in the kitchen." Irene's green eyes twinkled.

Dani followed her to the sunny room.

"Good morning, sweetie," her dad said. "Hungry? Did you sleep well? Feeling any better?"

"Yes to all."

"I hope the bed was comfortable."

"It was. Thanks, Irene."

Irene set a huge plate of pancakes, bacon, and fresh blueberries in front of her. "I'm happy to hear that. How about blueberry pancakes? I hope you're hungry."

"Mmm, smells good. Thank you." Dani sniffed the food, and Riley, who had been lying next to Dad, plodded over to Dani. "You've probably eaten a ton by now," she admonished him with a hug.

They talked about their plans, and Dad shared the timeline he'd devised with Irene.

"Good, then it's settled. You can move in here today."

She doesn't waste a minute. She wants us here. Dani shivered for some unknown reason.

"Well, Irene," Dad hesitated. "We really haven't been able to discuss that, Dani and I, I mean."

"But I thought it was all settled."

"Yes, it is." Dani smiled at her dad. "We are prepared to accept your offer. What's to discuss, Dad?" Her words surprised her, as if someone else were saying them.

Dad backed his chair from the table. "Really, Dani, you're okay with all this? Because yesterday you seemed rather negative. Maybe we need more time to—"

Irene cut him off. "Then it's settled. No worries. If any one of us wants to back out, we can. Let's give it a try, shall we?" She clapped like a child who had been given candy. "When can I expect you?"

"Well, we've been packing in anticipation of a move *somewhere*." Her dad studied her face. "Dani, a couple of days?"

Dani turned to Irene. "Sounds good to me."

"Then I'm delighted." She got up and hugged them both.

"Um, I have a concern," Dad piped up. "I have an extensive collection of paintings. They're small and medium size but still valuable. Would you allow me to hang them here, Irene? I don't want them sitting in storage. It's not good for paintings."

"Of course you may."

Wait until she sees them. Extensive *doesn't begin to describe it.*

"Mom and Dad loved to collect art. Original art. That's your motto, right? 'Always buy original.'"

"That's right, Dani. As long as they are noted artists and not prints. It adds to the value of the painting. I have a lot of Bucks County impressionists—Baum, Leith-Ross, Snell, and Coppedge, to name a few."

"I would love if you could share your knowledge with me, Ray, and together we can find the proper place to hang each one. Let's look in the parlor. That's a smaller room and in good shape. Perhaps they would fit nicely."

I'd be interested to take a second look at that room.

Dani followed them. Passing a huge gold-framed mirror, she did a double take. There was a white willowy swaying in it, as if it was alive. Pointing a finger, she whimpered at the mirror.

Irene and her dad rushed to the spot. "Dani, it's old glass. It bevels." Dad hugged her, trying to calm her by rationalizing.

"It's very old, Dani, an antique. You know, old glass can appear wavy and doesn't always project an accurate image. I really should throw it out. I don't think it's valuable at all. I'm sorry it frightened you." She put her arms around Dani.

"I saw him."

"Who, dear?"

"The boy in the album."

CHAPTER 12

Not What it Seems

Fall 1894

Nathan looked at his canvas. "I like to start with lathered thick brushstrokes of greens, blending the oils together to evoke the essence of trees foresting the countryside. This splendor of nature, Bernard, is the one place I'm content. It's perfect. When I paint it, I feel one with it and perfect too. Come, I'll teach you how the colors mesh to form objects."

Picking a thinner brush, he addressed the bulldog, who sat watching. "See how I swirl these into muted browns. I use various lengths and slender dashes to create a herd of white-tailed deer, adding puffs of white tail."

Bernard stretched and whined.

"Look. Quiet now or you'll scare them. Here's a biscuit and plenty more of those if you stay. That's it. Stay, Bernard. They're resting and feasting in the ravine. Lots of sweet grasses for them."

Bernard rested and watched as long as the biscuits kept coming.

"Incredible. What a reward," Nathan whispered. A flock of turkeys was waddling into the meadow in front of him. "Bernard, gorgeous colors. Have you ever seen anything like this? What, no response?" Bernard snorted and rested his head on his paws.

"I'm very happy we created our makeshift studio in the old springhouse. It's dry and deserted. The perfect place. Father never comes to these woods." Sighing, Nathan contemplated his sad relationship with his father.

He's become colder. He never was warm or interested in my painting. That's why I can only learn by practice. I wish I could take lessons, but he refuses to hire a tutor for that. I know I'm good, but I could be great with a little help. Why can't he see that I need help?

That made Nathan smile. His third tutor in five years was a lazy man of middle age who preferred to write rather than teach. The tutor would often accompany Nathan into the woods. Nathan could paint for hours, and the tutor would write.

"Ha, no one to really supervise us. Sarah wants me to be happy, so she won't say a word to Father."

Having no siblings and no way of meeting peers, Bernard and his tutor were his only companions for much of the day.

"I enjoy being alone, but Sarah asked Father for permission for me to go to a social at a church nearby. She wanted to escort me. She thought I should see people. Of course, he refused. He's much against fun, ye know, Bernard."

After several hours, he packed up his tubes of paint and carried his easel to the creek. He rested his canvas on the stone wall inside the little house to dry.

"Come, Bernard. It will be safe here. You may now romp to your heart's content."

He pulled the door shut, and they worked their way up the stony path to the open meadow. Bernard chased a rabbit to its hole and then focused on a butterfly.

"Ah, sticking to smaller game now? Those turkeys are too much for you."

On a previous outing, the turkeys had squawked viciously, hissing and trying to peck, so Bernard gave up and retreated to find something easier to engage in play.

"I'm lucky that Father permitted me to have you, Bernard. You're a rare breed, and most dogs aren't afforded the privilege of living indoors. I was sure that because Da sent you, Father would refuse to let me keep you, but he allowed it. Perhaps it was his guilt over not being here much. I prefer you anyway. He and I don't share any interests. I dread leaving you in two years for the bustling city. He plans to apprentice me in Philadelphia to learn his business of shipbuilding.

"Come, Bernard. We need to head home." They caught up to his tutor, who was writing on the cement table in the gardens.

"I was just going to fetch you, boy. Your father is here. Old James was sent by Sarah to make sure we return by dinner. I expect he'll want a full account of what you learned today."

"I can come up with some knowledge of the geography of the shipping lanes from here to London and South America. Think that will impress him?" They laughed, and his tutor patted Nathan on the back as they headed to the kitchen door of the manor.

"Why's he here?" Nathan questioned Sarah.

"No idea, young man, but let's not discuss painting, or some such, and rile him."

Nathan grinned and proceeded up the back stairs to his room to wash. "What do you think of this, Bernard?" He displayed a crisp white shirt in front of him. Bernard moved to sniff it. "Hey, none of your slobber on it." Pulling it away, he dressed in it, grabbed a pair of trousers, and headed down the stairs with the dog.

"I'm afraid it's the pantry for you, boy." He pushed the dog inside. "I'll be back." He headed to the dining room.

"Father, how good to see you." He extended his hand.

"It's nice that you address me as Father, Nathan, but you know that I am not your father. Please sit. Bow heads." They bowed their heads while the older man asked the blessing on their food.

"Mrs. Wythe." He rang a dinner bell. "You may serve."

"Yes, sir." Sarah presented them with a soup tureen with a steaming pumpkin puree. After the soup course was a large platter of pheasant, accompanied by carrots and steamed potatoes.

After a dinner in silence, the elder Hainsworth rang for Sarah.

"Mrs. Wythe, please bring coffee and your dessert and join us."

"Uh, begging your pardon, sir, join you?"

"Indeed. You will need to hear this as well."

Sarah poured coffee for the master and milk for Nathan and then sliced an apple pie. She joined them but did not partake of dessert or coffee. Folding her hands in front of her, she waited for the master to speak.

"I met with Mr. Joshua Barnaby today."

Nathan dropped his fork. Mrs. Wythe began to rub her fingers.

"He has agreed to take Nathan on for the next six months. He's developed a new initiative. We'll see how Nathan does with it."

"I believe I'll take a brandy in the parlor, Sarah, if there are no questions."

"But begging the master's pardon, sir, he's just a boy of fourteen."

"This meeting was to inform you, Mrs. Wythe, not to get your permission. It's been arranged. He'll leave next month."

Nathan clenched his fists and shouted, "No, no, I will not!"

"Excuse me?"

Nathan's whole body tensed in anger. Heart pounding, he screamed, "You have no right to do this!"

"Right? I have every right. You're my responsibility. Nathan sat glued to his seat, white- faced in rage.

"Sir," Mrs. Wythe tried again, plainly distressed at this turn of affairs. She sniffled into her hankie and teared up. "He's still a boy, sir. Perhaps more time. Losing his parents and brother was a terrible tragedy."

"He needs more than he's getting here, Sarah." He gently pushed back his chair. Pouring his own snifter of brandy, he headed to the parlor, followed by the two of them.

"And what if I refuse, Father?"

"The matter is settled, my boy. It's for your own good."

Nathan stormed out of the parlor and up the stairs.

CHAPTER 13

Summoned by the Spirit

The next day, Dani was remembering that mirror while she packed the last of her things. "I know what I saw, Riley." Riley whined. "I know Dad doesn't believe me. He tried to convince me that I had a fever and was hallucinating. It was the same boy as the one in the picture album in the library. Now he's not sure we should move to the manor, but I know that boy is trying to tell me something. I have to keep all talk of strange visions out of my conversations with Dad." She shook as she pulled the Ouija board from the back of her closet.

"Ready, Dani?" Dad called up to her. She stuffed the box into her backpack.

"If he had any clue what I'm thinking, he would never agree to the move to the mansion, Riley," she said and then called, "Be right down, Dad." She took the stairs two at a time.

"I'd like to have this rental back by dinner, if that's at all possible."

"Can Riley and I ride in the back?"

"I'd rather you didn't. You're safer up front with me. And I don't want that stained glass damaged."

A weird sensation came over her when he mentioned the stained glass window. *I almost forgot about the stained glass window.* "I always feel strange around that thing—and to think that I'm the one who wanted it," she whispered to herself.

"What was that?"

"Nothing, Dad. Just thinking out loud." She got in the front, and Riley hopped in beside her. Dani put on her EarPods and started humming to Lizzo, her favorite female recording artist.

In the middle of "Juice," she thought she heard something else. She pulled the pods out of her ears. Twice she heard an ominous voice whisper, "Unlock the secret."

"What's up?"

"Uh, nothing, Dad."

Minutes later, they arrived at the manor, greeted at the door by Irene.

"If you'll direct me, I'll unload and then we can unpack and relocate things later."

"Lovely plan, Ray."

"Irene, can I look through your library?" Dani was hoping to discover something about the boy and the bulldog. "Come with me, Ri." She was still shaking and unwilling to go anywhere in this house alone.

Irene hesitated, "Um, yes, I guess so, dear."

Why would she hesitate?

"Irene, I have this very valuable, fragile stained glass window. Where can I set it for the moment to keep it safe?"

That got Dani's attention. She needed to know where they were storing the stained glass window.

"It's safe in the library, Ray. Then we can find an appropriate place to hang it." Irene held the library door for him and pointed to a corner.

"It belongs to Dani. It's the first item she ever wanted to bid on."

"I know."

"You know?" Dani looked at her with raised eyebrows. Tensing, she asked, "What do you mean?"

Irene busied herself with securing the stained glass window to a spot on the rug. "I believe you mentioned this piece to me when we were discussing auctions." Irene's face turned pink. "What's next, Ray?" she called to him as she hurried from the room and out to the truck.

I never talked about this stained glass window with her. Dani watched Irene. *That was strange.*

She moved to the bookcase. "I need to ask her about that, Riley. I don't ever recall discussing the stained glass window." She paused. "Where is it? I know I got it from this shelf. Did I put it back on a different one?" Reading over every title, Dani realized the album was gone.

Irene moved it.

A murmur behind her made her turn. She froze. An icy breeze rustled the heavy drapes. Every inch of her body sensed a presence in the room. Voices from the hall told her that her dad and Irene were returning. The warmth in the room returned.

Shaking but unwilling to share this new occurrence with them, she turned back to the bookcase as they entered. "Oh." A family Bible lay open on the shelf in front of her.

"Dani, I hope it isn't too boring in here for you. We're almost done. You can plug your laptop in here, dear, and use this desk if you want to work on anything downstairs. I will give you the Wi-Fi password. I know how you young people love your technology."

"That's very sweet, Irene. I was wondering where that photo album is that I looked through a few days ago."

"We'll look for it later, dear. I would love it if you would help us make decisions on where to put things. After all, this will be your home too." Smiling, Irene glanced at the Bible and then held her arm out.

What choice do I have? Dani went with her to the hall.

Irene spent the rest of the afternoon with Dani in close proximity, making suggestions for lamps and small furniture that Ray claimed were priceless and he couldn't be without.

"This is a George Nakashima Conoid chair, Irene."

I'm sure Irene is clueless.

Dani thought she'd never have the chance to get back to the library, but Irene surprised her.

"Let's take a break, shall we? Dani, this might be a good time for you to resume your research in my library. I'll make some sandwiches."

I was sure she was keeping me from snooping. "Thank you, Irene. Come on, Riley."

But when Dani scanned the shelves in the library, there was no sign of the open Bible or the photo album.

How did she do that? Irene was with me every second this afternoon. Dani searched again. *Not here.* Standing with arms akimbo, she perused the bookcase. Out of the corner of her eye, she saw something twinkle.

The quilts covering the stained glass window were in a heap on the floor. Shuddering, she tried to remain in her spot, but the glass summoned her. The thick velvet drapes prevented light from outside, but the colors in the glass sparkled as if it were alive. Whispers emanated from it: "Unlock the secret."

Dani tried to ignore it. "There's nothing there. It's my imagination."

A voice emanated from the glass: "You must unlock the secret."

CHAPTER 14

The Ghost Emerges

Her dad's voice from the hall broke the spell. The glass went dark, the room quiet. Pages fluttered. She gazed behind her at the bookcase. The photo album was open.

"Riley." Clutching her arms to her chest, she moved with him toward the bookcase. Hands shaking, she reached out to look through it.

"Honey, Irene has some lunch for us. What are you doing?"

"I-I'm … We were about to look through this album." She couldn't tell him. He would never believe her—probably rush her off to a psych ward. "I'm not really hungry."

"Just come sit, then. Irene went to a lot of trouble."

Yeah, I'll bet. She's going to a lot of trouble to have us here. Why? Is Irene part of all this strangeness? Or is the stained glass window the reason?

"Sure, Dad. Coming."

Dani couldn't eat a bite of food, but by the time lunch was over, calm had descended on her.

"Let's continue our work. There are spaces for your paintings in the great room, Ray."

By the end of the day, Dani had been in a half dozen rooms of various sizes, rooms that she hadn't seen on their initial visit.

"This place goes on forever, Irene. Oh, is that a Garber?"

"I'm impressed, Dani. It is. I don't know that I'd recognize a Garber if I hadn't known it was one. It belonged to a distant cousin, I think. It came with the house."

"It's beautiful. I love the Bucks County impressionist painters." Dani gaped, remarking at the painting filling a whole wall of the great room.

"I do as well. In fact, I have several—but none as fine as yours, Irene. That one is worth millions," Dad added.

"I appreciate its beauty. I hope I never have to part with it."

While they were talking about paintings and the countryside, a meadow came into Dani's mind's eye. She could envision being there.

"What's wrong, Dani?"

"Um, nothing, Dad. Why?"

"You have a weird look on your face."

I don't want him to think I'm still hearing voices or imagining things.

"Just thinking about art." *God, does that sound lame!* Changing the subject, she picked up the Fern Coppedge and looked around. "Where could we hang this? She's the most known female artist of the Bucks County painters and is one of my favorites. See how vibrant her colors are compared to some others?"

"My, you do know quite a bit, Dani."

Hours flew by as Dani imparted what knowledge she had

about each of her dad's paintings. "I feel like each artist is in the house with me."

"That's how I feel, Dani, but you never said that before." Dad looked at her, reaching out to hug her.

"I guess I'm realizing it." She hugged him back.

"Look at the time. We've accomplished a good deal." Irene ran her fingers through her white hair. "How about a cup of tea?"

"I'd love one, Irene." Dad set his toolbox down, following her to the kitchen.

"Can I call Madisen?" Dani asked, trailing behind them.

"That's a lovely idea. Invite her over."

"Really, Irene?" *She's full of surprises.*

"I'm looking forward to meeting your friends, and they should see your new home. What about this weekend?"

"Dad?" She looked at her father.

"Fine   with   me.   It's   Irene's   house."
"It's *our* house, Ray." Smiling, she set the kettle on the stove.

Dani took her cell to the library. She needed to share with Madisen. Crazy thoughts were still filling the back of her head, but she was sure Madisen would know what to say to her. They FaceTimed for half an hour.

"I'm sorry for the way things were between us, Dani."

"It's over, Madisen. We'll always be friends, no matter what."

"I was nasty to you. Friends don't do that."

"It was scary for you—and for me. When you can't explain something, it can be scary," Dani said.

"It won't happen again. I'm here for you."

But will you understand when I tell you that I continue to have these experiences?

They hung up after mapping out a plan for the weekend. Dani thought she might have to see Dr. Robin if things continued. Madisen hadn't had any explanations.

She told Irene and Dad she was finishing some unpacking in her room, and she and Riley went up the back stairs to the second floor.

"I forgot about this." She pulled the Ouija board out of her backpack and slid it under the bed.

"Maybe Madisen would like to have some fun with this this weekend, Riley."

The photo album popped back into her head, so she took Riley and tiptoed back down the front staircase to the library. *No need to alert Irene or Dad. I can't trust Irene yet. There's something strange about her behavior.*

Entering the library, Dani shuddered as icy air engulfed her. *Maybe Dad will make a fire later.*

The stained glass window stood in the same place. She surprised herself as to how calm she felt now.

"At least it hasn't moved, Riley. Let's look at the album before anyone discovers us here."

She found several albums she hadn't seen before, gathered them up, and snuggled on the couch under an afghan with Riley. "Look at this, Riley. There aren't any names, but this album has pictures of a baby, a little boy, and a teenager, but then it stops. And there are no pictures of adults."

A feeling of sadness engulfed her. The room closed in on her, and she sensed a presence again.

The canine whined and then jumped off the couch, snarling at the stained glass window. "Riley, get back here."

A boy of about sixteen was materializing out of the glass. His collarless white shirt with long puffy sleeves contrasted with the darkness of his eyes, which were smiling at her through their sadness. An equally forlorn-looking bulldog accompanied him.

He's not dressed like any of the boys around here.

"Don't be afraid." His voice was gentle and soothing.

Opening her mouth to speak, the voice that came out was shaky and small. "Who are you? What do you want?" She stood before the stained glass window.

The filmy creature beckoned in response, and Dani and Riley floated through the air, out the french doors, and in an instant landed in front of the springhouse. The vine-covered door was open. She moved on her own now and crept into the dwelling, following the gesturing boy and bulldog.

An artist's easel and a tin of paint tubes stood in the little house. Then Dani heard voices. "Dani, Dani." Her father's voice broke her trance.

Kneeling, he scooped her up off the cold stone. "What are you doing here? We've been searching for hours. The french doors were open, and Riley was barking and snarling for us to follow him. If he hadn't summoned us, we may never have found you."

But Riley was with me.

Dani was too cold and weak to offer an explanation. Her last memory was of the forlorn faces of the young boy and bulldog begging her to follow them.

"Let's get her to the manor." Irene wrapped a warm blanket around her. "We can get the whole story after some hot milk and a nice fire."

Sounds good to me. Dani relaxed, comforted in her father's arms.

Voices again filled her sleeping mind, but this time she awoke in the library on the leather sofa, in front of a cozy fireplace. The voices were her dad's and Irene's.

"Hi, honey. You're waking up. How about some milk or warm cocoa?"

"Um, cocoa sounds good, Dad."

"You got it."

In minutes, he returned with it, setting it in front of her. Dad sat close beside her. "Ready to talk, honey? What were you doing so far out in the woods without a jacket and without telling us?"

Dani took a deep breath, looking to Irene for support. "The boy and the bulldog in the album came to me—out of the stained glass window, Dad. Don't ask me how. I don't know …"

It was Dad's turn to take a deep breath. "Dani, look—"

"Dad, you have to believe me," she interrupted him, her voice loud at this point.

"I'm sure you *think* you saw you saw someone. We've been hanging paintings …"

"That's what he wanted me to find in the springhouse, his easel and paints. I don't know why he wanted us to find the paints …"

"Dani, Irene and I didn't see any easel or paints, right, Irene?" He looked to her for affirmation, but she gave a weak look and held her chin. "You saw the album and then maybe sleepwalked. We're all tired and emotional. I shudder to think what would have happened to you in those woods overnight. Thank God for Riley."

"Riley flew with us. He was in the springhouse with me."

"Yes, well, he must have come back to get us when you fainted. No more talk of flying through the air—and boys and bulldogs from the stained glass window. Tomorrow we are calling Dr. Robin and having some tests run. This all has a logical explanation. Now it's after midnight. We need to put you to bed."

"What? But it was early, right after dinner."

"Exactly. That's what we're telling you. You've been in the cold woods for hours."

Dani shook her head, now in tears. "I don't understand. Dad, I can't go to sleep right now. I'm afraid." Dani knew she wasn't scared, just confused. She wanted to talk about it with someone and sort out the details. But not Dad.

"Irene, would you sit with me in my room and talk?"

"Oh, uh, yeah, honey. I guess Irene would be more comforting." Dad seemed uncomfortable.

Irene was sitting across from her all this time, watching Dani and chewing on a nail. "Yes, of course, Dani. I don't know what to make of this, but I know we'll figure it all out."

"Well, I guess I'll say good night here. Call me if you need me." Her dad retired to his bedroom, and Irene asked Dani to start from the beginning and tell her the details. Dani had a hunch that there was more to Irene than she was letting them see.

"If this *is* a spirit, you must not go with him again. It could be dangerous." Surprised at Irene's advice, Dani listened, brows knitted.

"You believe me, then, don't you, Irene?" Dani looked at Irene, eyes wide. "I wasn't afraid of him. I sort of felt sorry for him and the bulldog. They needed Riley and me, but I'm not sure why. I'm sure that I can't control not going. Something compels me to follow."

"Of course I believe you. We need to find out who this spirit is and what he wants. I'm not sure how we're going to do that, but I have an idea. When you think he's contacting you, tell him to go away. If you're adamant enough and use your strongest voice, maybe he won't feel welcome."

"All right. I'll try that." Dani felt comforted to know that at least Irene believed her.

The next morning, Dani was compelled by a different spirit, her father, to eat toast and fruit, and then accompany him to see Dr. Robin.

She always enjoyed seeing Dr. Robin. The perky brown-haired woman was always cheery and smiling, and no matter how sick Dani could be, she was comforted by Dr. Robin's professional, gentle manner. Today was no different, and the advice she offered helped to validate Dani's feelings.

"You're trying to be brave, Dani, but you need to let your feelings out. You've been through a horrible time losing your mom, and you need to talk about it. And crying is okay."

Dr. Robin hugged her and assured her that therapy would help, telling her, "Think of it being like a hug, a cup of soothing honey tea, and someone to listen to you while you vent."

After their visit, Dani felt less anxious.

"What did Dr. Robin tell *you*?" Dani asked.

Dad patted her hand as they drove home. "She assured me that therapy will help you talk out your fears. She thinks that it's lasted longer than a normal six-month grieving period and maybe a mild medication would be good too. She gave me the names of several counselors. I guess I underestimated your grief. We're going to spend more time together too."

Dani said nothing, just heaved a sigh. Finally, she said, "I have a counselor at school."

"I think it might be a little more involved than seeing the school counselor, honey."

Dani's eyes filled, but she refused to be wimpy. *I'm not crazy. You'll all see.*

CHAPTER 15

The Ouija Moved

Saturday morning arrived, and Dani woke excited to spend the weekend with Madisen. Her plan was to go to the springhouse and find the easel and paints. *I hope I can make Madisen see what I'm seeing. I don't want her to think I'm insane.*

"I have a great idea," Dad announced as he folded his paper when Dani entered the kitchen.

"Good morning to you too, Dad," she said, seating herself at the table.

"I'm sorry, sweetheart. Here, give me a kiss." He patted her cheek. "I've been thinking about maybe following a routine for a few weeks. Since school has begun, we're all having earlier evenings and mornings, homework, relax time, and so on. Let's make a schedule and put it here in the kitchen so we all know each other's plans. Mom used to keep a chart on the kitchen wall, remember, Dani?"

"That sounds, lovely, Ray," Irene responded.

Not to me. This is Dad's way of keeping tabs on me.

"Yeah, Dad, sounds like a plan." Dani could fill in what she wanted him to know and leave out the rest.

"Great. I'll pick up a nice chart when I'm out today. I have a full day of ordering and picking up renovation supplies, but since Madisen will be here, I hope you won't mind that I'm not around. What time are we expecting her?"

"Her mom is dropping her off this morning." She glanced at the clock just as the doorbell rang. "In fact, that's probably her." Dani went to the front door. She waved to Mrs. Campbell in the car.

"Nice digs, Dani. I'd love a tour sometime," Madisen's mother called.

"Sure thing, Mrs. C. Anytime." She grabbed Madisen's hand, leading her to the kitchen.

"I want you to meet Mrs. Monaghan. Mrs. Monaghan, this is my friend Madisen."

"Very nice to have you here, Madisen. I hope you girls will keep yourselves busy this morning. I'll give you the grand tour this afternoon. I have errands to do first."

Dad gave Madisen a hug and excused himself. Dani took this opportunity to try to convince Irene to stay away from the manor as long as she needed to.

"Irene, I know you have a lot to do. I can show Madisen around. Then you will have time to yourself before dinner."

"If you're sure, Dani. I do have quite a list, and I'd appreciate the time." Irene left them alone.

"We're going to the springhouse. And you can't tell my father."

"What? What springhouse? No, no, Dani, not that same ..."

"Please, listen, Madisen. You have to believe me. And see for yourself."

She related the events leading up to finding the easel and paints, including the photo album.

"If the easel and paints were there, why are we going to look for them now?"

"I haven't been back there, and Dad and Irene said they didn't see them. The boy wanted me to find them. They hold a secret. There's a connection between them and the old man, but I don't know what."

Later they talked as they approached the woods. Madisen glanced behind her. "There's someone watching us from the tower window."

Dani stopped and looked back but saw nothing. "You saw that too?"

"Yes, is it Irene?"

"Not likely. Irene was with my dad and me when I saw it. It's boarded up, and Irene says no one else lives here."

"Dani, you know how I feel about ghosts. I'm not comfortable with this."

Dani crossed her arms and confronted her. "If you don't believe in ghosts, Madisen, then what's the problem?"

"I don't want to get in trouble for disobeying your dad, and there could be real danger from real people. Bad people."

Dani continued down the path, ignoring her and calling back, "Tell me if you think it's the same springhouse."

Madisen gasped. "That's it. Let's go back, Dani. It's dark in these woods."

"Look, we'll get the easel and paints and take them back to the manor to see if they provide any clues. I need to know who this boy is and why he's contacting me."

They approached the little house, and a soft glimmer of light shone from inside. Dani's heart pounded in her chest.

"Dani, please."

Dani could hear Madisen's voice pleading with her to leave, but she was powerless to move. A musty odor assailed her nose as she entered the springhouse.

"The diary. Take the diary." The words echoed through the stone house. A bloodcurdling scream that sounded like Madisen's voice came from outside. Dani tried to turn to leave, but her feet held fast to the stone.

She screamed as an icy hand grabbed her from behind. "It's me, silly. Didn't you hear me screaming for you to come out? All kinds of weird filmy fog filled that house, and I couldn't open the door. It was locked tight."

"But the voice ..."

"What voice? I didn't hear any voices. Filmy fog—that's all. And that's enough for me. Let's go."

They ran back to the manor and slipped in the french doors to the library in order to avoid Irene if she was home. Once upstairs, safe in Dani's room, she directed Madisen to lock the door quickly.

Madisen saw part of the box sticking out from under Dani's bed. She pulled out the Ouija board.

"I have an idea. Let's contact this boy spirit who is stalking me. I don't really know how to use it. Do you?" Dani asked.

"I watched a scary movie once where they conjured up all kinds of ghouls," Madisen offered. "But it was just a movie."

"Maybe we should wait until everyone's asleep." Dani set it down on the floor, and the planchette made a figure eight.

"It moved ...all by itself," Dani whispered.

"That's not good." Madisen grabbed Dani's hand. "I only know one thing about the Ouija board."

Dani interrupted. "Maybe the boy is trying to contact us."

Dani put her hands on the planchette. "Who are you?"

It spelled out *NH*.

"Are you the boy with the bulldog?"

The planchette pointed to *yes*.

"Springhouse!" a voice shouted, scaring the girls. As they grabbed each other, the planchette flew off the board.

"Let's go." Dani stood up.

"What? Where?" Madisen asked, still shuddering in fear.

"The springhouse, of course. No one is home. Let's see what it wants us to find."

"Ohhh," Madisen whined, but she reluctantly followed Dani.

They ran through the woods to the small house. The door was now ajar. "You wait here and stand guard with Riley," Dani said.

A bright light illuminated a crevice in the wall. Dani sailed to it and pulled a small package wrapped in animal hide from it. She unwrapped it. It held a leather-bound book stamped with gold initials. "It's a journal. This is the diary that the voice was telling me about." Dani noticed another packet wrapped in skins protruding from a crevice in the stone wall. "Wait, what's this?" She reached in and pulled it out, opening several canvases. She headed out the door.

"Look at this, Madisen. What does this mean?" The paintings were all black, red, and deep purples depicting daggers dripping with blood, dead animals, and bodies of dead people. The painting was very juvenile and suggested art painted by a severely disturbed young child. We have to take it back and hide it from my dad and Irene. Tonight we'll read it when we're alone.

***

"How horrid. Who could have painted these?" Madisen asked.

"I don't know, but let's go. We'll figure it out later."

They returned to her room and placed the Ouija flat, with the planchette on top. Dani tried to put her hands on it, but the planchette moved on its own. It made another figure eight.

"That's the one thing I remember about Ouija boards," Madisen said. "A figure eight means a wicked soul has power over the board."

CHAPTER 16

An Unwelcome Change

1894, *Spring*

I am trying to adjust to my new life in Philadelphia. Gone are the rolling green meadows of Bucks County. My room is in a three-story old shambles of a building. Knowing Father as I do, he revels in making my accommodations simple and rough. My wages are meager, but then, I don't want for anything except paints. Since I am not permitted home for three months, I have all weekend to paint. I will go to the river. I find the swirling of the moving water both calming and exhilarating.

A knock on his door startled him, and he put his diary away. "It's Saturday, Mr. Nathan. I'm sure you're looking forward to your excursion by the Schuylkill."

"Oh, it's you. Yes, I'll be meeting my artist friends there."

"Ah, so you will, sir. After some food, we'll leave. I've got the buggy ready."

He thought about his days here as they rolled along toward the river. *I do miss Bernard and Sarah Wythe terribly. The shipping industry holds no excitement for me, and I find myself daydreaming of the beauty of nature that has been stolen from me. The city smells and is one color: charcoal. The factories rise depressingly poor. It's not the lack of comfort that I mind ... or the blandness of food. It's the brilliance of color that is lacking in my life here.*

Morning had dawned, and light streamed into his tiny room. Nathan stared at the ceiling and watched a spider build a web across one beam to another. His attic abode chilled him, and he dressed to head to the kitchen for a bowl of porridge. He guessed by the light that it would be approaching seven and he should be up. He was happy that it was Saturday and he had a free day.

"I'll wait here for you until after your repast, sir."

He sat at a long wooden table able to accommodate the six boarders who let rooms. This morning he ate alone, without benefit of the conversation of Mrs. Wythe or her good food, not to mention the comfort and love afforded him by Bernard. He gathered his dish and spoon and washed it in the sink, collected his cap, and headed outside.

June 3, 1894

A marvelous miracle happened. While sketching in Fairmount Park in the city, I happened upon a group of artists. They study at the Pennsylvania Academy of Art and Design. Their instructor, Professor Anshutz introduced himself. After some conversation, I let him know that I paint oil and watercolors of landscapes. I showed him a rolled canvas that I had with me. He liked my work. I'm overjoyed. I've been invited to bring a sandwich and join them on Saturdays.

Nathan continued his journal entries, documenting his joy at painting, sadness at being away from Sarah Wythe and Bernard, and misery at being forced to learn the shipbuilding industry.

February 4, 1895

Professor Anshutz imparted many new techniques to me. I've learned to manipulate paint colors to suggest light or shadows. I enjoy being with this "Group of Ten," as they call themselves. I have accumulated many canvases of the Schuylkill River.

"Now there, stay over here in your area."

"But I need to paint from this angle." Nathan felt his anger rising. He needed to be closer to the water, and this oaf was preventing him.

The professor approached him and told him how much better he was than the others. Nathan was thrilled, but it didn't change his mind. "I'm taking my easel and paints on the other side."

The oaf grabbed him by the arm, knocking over his canvas, sending it into the mire.

"Fool, now look what you've done." He watched as his friends picked up his things and helped him into the buggy. Painting was finished for today.

Returning to his room at his boardinghouse, he was met by

Mr. Barnaby. "Young Nathan, I am seeing to it that you are sent home. You cannot stay here."

I'm delighted. I'm to go on holiday back to the mansion in Bucks County. I've done so well here.

CHAPTER 17

More Secrets

"How do you know so much?"

"I read about it online, and everything I read was serious. It isn't a toy."

"OMG, Dani. Of course it's a toy. You can buy it online, under toys. It used to be in Toys "R" Us under games, silly. But after what we saw, I believe you. Let's put it back under your bed. Besides I'd rather read the diary." Madisen bent to slide it into the box and the planchette fell off.

"Madisen …," Dani scolded.

"What? It isn't broken." Madisen packed it into the box slowly, as if to convince Dani that she was being careful. "I think we should do something totally different."

Dani gave her a weak smile. "Sorry, I don't care if it gets broken. I mean, I just don't want it to do anything bad."

"No worries," Madisen said.

"But we're both worried. I can't really read the diary right now. I'm not ready for any more surprises just yet."

"Dinner!" Irene's voice summoned them to the kitchen, where Dani's dad greeted them.

"Hey, ladies, how was your day? What did you two do?"

Dani shot Madisen a look.

"Dani showed me the property. It's great, Irene. I love all the trees and flower gardens. Didn't see the whole mansion yet."

Dani mouthed, "Thank you."

They conversed throughout dinner in the kitchen and then went to the formal dining room, where Irene and Dad elaborated on some new plans.

"You should try to find a brass chandelier like the original one," Dani said, chiming into the conversation. The place where the light fixture hung was a huge hole and a mess of wires.

"Dani, how do you know a brass chandelier hung here?" Her dad knitted his brow.

"Um, maybe I saw it in one of the albums."

"Oh, well, if we can find one. What do you think, Irene?"

Turning to Irene, they all saw her facial expression register fright.

"Irene, is something wrong?" Dad went toward her.

"No, not at all. I was just looking at all the work involved in this one room alone; it's staggering."

Really? I don't believe you, Irene. You had a look of horror on your face. Did you see something on that ceiling?

"We know there's a phenomenal amount of work. We're prepared to tackle it too. One day at a time." Dad reached out and hugged Irene. "No need to worry." He stood, hands on hips, and surveyed the room. "I promise you we will restore this manor to the showplace it was once. And you know what, Dani? You and Madisen can help."

"How?" they asked in unison.

"You mentioned that you saw a picture of this room. You

could provide Irene and me with details of the furniture, paint, wallpaper, and various other decor from that time period. It would sure save us the work of researching all that. Irene?"

"Oh, yes, that would be lovely." Her monotone betrayed that she wasn't sure. "It's getting late. If we want to play a board game before bed, we should start now." She turned and headed out of the room.

"What do you want to play, Madisen? Since you're our guest, you get to choose," Dad said.

"Hmm, how about Clue?"

"Yes," Dani piped up, "that's one of my favorites."

"Okay, ladies," Dad announced after several hours, "I think I'm exhausted and ready to turn into bed."

"It's not a school night, Dad. Can Madisen and I stay up? I'm not sleepy."

"I guess so, but not too late. You need lots of sleep."

"I believe I'll retire too and read in bed for a bit." Irene said. She and Dad bid them good night, and Dani and Madisen headed for the library.

"What do you what to do in the library?" Madisen asked. "I thought we were going to read the diary."

"I wanted to see if I could find any identification to go with the photo of the boy and the bulldog," Dani replied.

They paged through an album with old photos.

"Look, there's a portrait on the wall in this picture of a room. What room is this?"

"I'm not sure, Madisen. There are many little sitting rooms on this floor and the second level. I haven't been in all of them yet."

"This portrait has two people and a dog. But it's so old."

"That does look like a bulldog. Let's get the diary. I need to read it." Dani stood up and started through the library door.

"Aren't we supposed to be looking for pictures of rooms in this place?"

"That can wait," Dani whispered. "This is more important."

They crept up the dimly lit center hall stairs to the second floor.

This place is eerie," Madisen said. "I'd reconsider if I were you and your dad. I like it during the day but not at night."

"I know, but now I feel invested in solving this boy's problem and the connection to this mansion." Dani noticed that Madisen shivered at her adamant response.

Once in Dani's room, the girls locked the door and retrieved the diary.

"Does this gold initial mean anything to you, Dani?"

"No." Dani opened to the first page and began reading aloud. "Wait. The initial," Dani said, remembering. "*N* was one of the initials the Ouija board gave us."

Her voice was interrupted by a thundering bang in the hall. Dani screamed and hugged Madisen, who seemed too terrified to find her voice. Riley growled at the door. The booming noise was coming closer, and then it stopped outside her room.

"It stopped," Madisen whispered.

"Let's look in the hall."

"No, are you crazy, Dani? I'm not going out there."

Despite her protest, she clung to Dani and moved when she did. They approached the door, slowly opening it and gazing into an empty hall.

"It's him." Dani left Madisen and headed toward the stairs.

"No, Dani, come back. Don't go down there."

Dani went to the library. The door was open, and she could see the stained glass window. She moved toward it, and as she did, a whirling swirl of color materialized into a young boy dressed in clothes from the past.

"I told you to read the diary. You must obey me."

Dani's lips were moving. Then the green glow in the room disappeared.

"Dani, are you all right?"

"I'm fine, Madisen. He needs my help."

"Who? Who needs your help? We have to tell your dad about this—now."

"No, we can't. Please, Madisen, let's try to Google information about this mansion."

The girls spent several hours on each of their phones, trying to find facts related to the mansion using only the address.

"This is futile," Dani said. "There's nothing on Google— except that the mansion exists. Tomorrow we're going to clean the crud off the bottom of this stained glass window and then go to use the Bucks County Historical Library of the Mercer Museum. Maybe we can find out some more history about this place."

⁓

Dani and Madisen were so anxious to solve the identity of the boy that despite the fact that they were up late, they arose early and both went down to the kitchen to the smells of breakfast.

"But, Dad …" Dani presented her argument, trying to convince him. "Everybody walks into downtown. I'm thirteen. I'm not a baby. And Madisen will be with me." She shot Madisen a glance.

"Oh, yeah, Mr. R. We'll stay on the sidewalks and be really careful."

"You're still thirteen, young lady. And I don't like it. It's at least a mile from here."

"Dad, puh-leeze. It's less than a mile, and it's all sidewalks."

Ray gave Irene a questioning look. She winked, nodded, and smiled.

"Well, okay. But text me when you get there. And when you leave. And don't talk to strangers and—"

"We get it, Dad. Thank you, thank you, and thank you. You won't be sorry. We'll be back by four for Madisen's mom."

Irene laughed. "You keep adding details for them, Ray. Just let them go. They're both reliable young ladies."

"Wait. What is it you're going to do in town?" Dani's dad raised his eyebrows.

"They have a new interactive exhibit at Mercer." Dani lied so smoothly that she was beginning to worry herself. She was going to Mercer Museum, but not for the exhibit.

On their way, she confided to Madisen. "My dad would freak if he thought I was doing research on this property ... and about that ghost of a boy and dog."

Once inside, they took the elevator to the library.

"I've never been in this section of the museum. This gives me the creeps." Madisen was walking so close to Dani that she stepped on her shoes several times.

"I guess it is weird. There are so many old artifacts up here, but it also holds tons of information. There are old deeds, records, and books from the sixteen hundreds. They told us about the library on a field trip in sixth grade. Anyone can use it, and I hope we can find stuff about the mansion—maybe the original deed and birth, death, and marriage records."

Once they arrived, the woman in charge of the library greeted them. "Hello, ladies. What can I do to help you?" She introduced herself as Rayna and spent several minutes orienting them to all the documents.

"Wow," Dani replied. "This is so cool. I didn't know you had all these."

"Yes, we have loads of original documents on these microfilm reels and microfiche."

"What's this thing?" She was referring to a big desk-like thing with alphabetized drawers.

Rayna laughed. "I guess that would be unfamiliar to you. It's called a card catalog."

Rayna explained how to use the card catalog and all the other equipment, and the girls began their research.

"Look at this."

"What does this mean, Dani?"

"Come on, this information is a great find." Wide-eyed, Dani smiled. "Let's make copies. And let's keep this quiet until I figure out what it means, okay?"

The newspaper article from the 1896 edition of *The Intelligencer* revealed the name of the mansion and some details about the tragedies that befell the original owners.

Back at the mansion, Dani helped Madisen retrieve her things and waited with her for her mom to arrive.

"I wish you could stay overnight so we could read the diary together."

"Yeah, me too."

She doesn't sound happy about spending another night.

"Well, here's my mom."

"Let's plan something soon." They hugged tightly.

"Hey, you're choking me." Dani laughed. "We're not parting forever."

"Be careful, Dani. Please. And text me tonight."

"I will. Don't sound so ominous."

Madisen got in the car and waved goodbye, her brows knitted in a frown.

"Gosh, what's with her, huh, Riley? Let's go see if we can find a way to clean that inscription without Irene seeing us."

Irene was engrossed in some reading project of her own, so Dani offered to dust and vacuum the library to give her an excuse to be in there.

"Now I won't look suspicious with cleaning supplies, Ri."

She set to work scrubbing the rest of the inscription. Unlike the other times that she tried to reveal a name, this time, for some unknown reason, she was able to uncover the inscription, which read "Nathan Hainsworth."

CHAPTER 18

Steel-Gray Eyes

"Hey, sweetie." Dad peeked into the library. "How was your day with Madisen?"

Before Dani could answer, he exclaimed, "Wow, this room is sparkling. You two did a fine job. Irene will be so happy when she sees it."

"Thanks, Dad." She noticed that he hadn't glanced at the stained glass and so he missed the inscription. "We had a great day. How about you?"

"It was busy. That's for sure. I'll fill you in over dinner. Get your hands washed and meet me in the kitchen. I think I smell something good."

They shared their stories of each one's day but Dani withheld most of hers.

After dinner, Dani begged to be excused, claiming that she wanted to read a new book she got from the library. She actually couldn't wait to get her hands on the diary. Sitting at the desk in her bedroom, she thought it would be smart to hide the diary inside her library book, just in case her dad or Irene came into her room.

January 1895

I want so much to be an artist. I live to create images on paper. The colors in the paints mesmerize as I try to duplicate the colors in the landscapes. One splash of color becomes a marvelous likeness to my subject. And this beautiful Bucks County countryside never disappoints. I never want to leave here.

Dani read for some time, fascinated by this account, wondering what kind of person wrote these words. Hearing her dad's footsteps on the stairs, she hid the diary.

"Come in, Dad," she said, answering his tap on the door.

"Getting late, honey. That book must be fascinating."

"Yes, it is. I was just about to get my jammies on."

"Then you get ready and I'll be back to tuck you in." Dad smiled and coaxed Riley off her bed.

"I'll let Ri out for a minute and be back."

Dani changed into her pajamas and went to brush her teeth. Musing about the passage she'd just read, she thought how lucky she was to have her dad. It sounded from the diary that Nathan had a very cold, uncaring father. With his mother dead, the entries revealed the feelings of a very unhappy young man. A sudden frigid breeze snapped her to attention. Her toothbrush still in her mouth, she saw the reflection of a gaunt-faced old man with icy gray eyes. She dropped the brush. The man pointed a bony finger at her, and the words, *Be careful*, appeared on her mirror. The young boy appeared. The apparitions disappeared at the same time, and the icy cold room was restored to normal temperature.

She could hear Riley snarling and barking. "Dani, Dani, open this door," her dad said.

"Oh my goodness, Dani, please let us in." Irene banged on the door.

After what seemed like forever, Dani heard a key turn in the lock.

"Dani, what's wrong? I've never heard such horrific sounds," her dad said.

Toothbrush hanging from her mouth, Dani was shivering in fear. Irene and her dad surrounded her, enfolding her in their arms. Irene's soothing voice calmed her.

"Dani, why was your door locked?"

Before she could answer, her dad asked, "What's this?"

He found the diary, which had slipped out of Dani's book in the melee and now lay at the bottom of her bed.

"It's a diary. It belongs to the boy, the one I saw with the bulldog. He wants me to read it and help him. He can't rest at peace until I find out the secret and expose it."

"Where did you get this, Dani?" her dad asked.

"The boy led me to it." Dani tried not to tell him that she disobeyed him and went to the springhouse.

"With the bizarre noises coming from your room and the locked door, we thought someone was in here hurting you. I told you there are to be no locked doors." Ray's hands flailed in front of himself.

"I didn't lock the door. The demon did." Dani began to sob.

"This apparition demon nonsense. Dani, I don't know what to do." Ray threw his hands in the air.

"I want the light on. I can't sleep. I'm afraid the demon will come back," Dani whimpered.

"Ray, she's hysterical, scared to death. Please go warm some milk and I'll try to soothe her fears. Dani, let's sit on the sofa in the library until you're sleepy."

Dani was amazed at Irene's tranquil behavior. She took control of the situation, even ordering her dad to the kitchen, and he did her bidding. But Dani noticed that he took the diary with him.

"Thank you, Irene." Dani, shaky still, allowed Irene to help her into her robe and guide her downstairs to the library. Seated on the loveseat with Riley and waiting for the milk, Irene looked up and gasped.

"The stained glass window … the inscription. You can read the name."

"Oh, I cleaned it all off today. I was going to ask you if the name meant anything to you."

Irene walked over to the stained glass window, and Dani sat on the edge of the sofa, keenly interested now and much calmer.

"My ancestors were Hainsworths. This mansion and all the grounds used to be called Hainsworth Manor. My distant cousin, maybe fourth or fifth generation, was Josiah Hainsworth, the owner. Nathan Hainsworth was his son."

Dani shivered. "Irene, the initials on the diary my dad took from me are NH. Nathan Hainsworth? You have to get it back for me. I need to read it."

Her dad returned with the milk, looking exhausted but talking in a softer voice.

"Ray, Dani cleaned the inscription and discovered the name on the stained glass window." She went on to explain the connection to her ancestors.

"I don't care what name is on it. It's a coincidence. I want the whole thing dropped, forgotten, and not pursued again. Am I understood? Finish your milk, Dani, and I will tuck you in. Are you about ready to try to sleep?"

She nodded but really didn't want to go to sleep. She was still fearful of that horrible-looking man.

Dad continued. "Reading that diary caused you to have a nightmare." Dani watched as he placed the diary on one of the top shelves of the bookcase. "Let's get you tucked in. No reading. Go right to sleep."

But sleep did not come. About an hour later, she heard a soft tap on her door.

"Are you awake, dear?" Irene opened the door a crack.

"Yes."

Irene shut the door behind herself. "I want you to know that I believe you, Dani. There must be something in the diary that explains why the boy is trying to contact you. I want to help you, but I don't want to anger your father. I'd rather he not know."

Dani was raised to not keep secrets. She was astounded that Irene was suggesting they keep secrets from her dad, but she had no choice. Irene was willing to get the diary for her and help her figure out what the boy wanted.

"Thank you, Irene." They hugged, and Dani snuggled back under the covers.

"Now try to sleep, dear." Irene smiled and left.

This is an interesting twist, Dani mused.

CHAPTER 19

The Tower Room

orning sun streamed through Dani's window. Waking fully, the terror of the night before filled her mind.

Was there a demon out to hurt Nathan? Why? Taking a deep breath, she resolved to forget her own welfare and try to help the boy.

Padding down to the kitchen in her slippers, with Riley at her side, she found her dad reading the paper and eating sausages.

Irene winked at her. "Good morning, Dani. What would you like for breakfast?"

"Hi, Irene. I'm not very hungry yet." She glanced at her dad, who lowered his paper.

Clearing his throat, he spoke. "I owe both of you an apology for my behavior last night. That ungodly noise and the locked door scared me so much that I let my fear for Dani's welfare cloud my good manners. I'm sorry. By the way, what made that noise? Did you have your iPod turned up on some crazy channel, Dani?"

Dani smiled at his lack of technical knowledge and weakly uttered, "No, Dad. I don't remember, maybe."

"Well, let's try to forget the whole thing happened and enjoy this wonderful breakfast Irene has made for us."

It was uncanny how Dad could just pretend that last night never happened. But he did. Breakfast was uneventful, and no one talked about the previous evening.

"I'll be working in the west wing, where I'm interviewing several potential subcontractors."

"And I have errands to run," Irene announced.

"I have to finish a summer reading project."

"I guess we all have our day mapped out for us."

They all finished breakfast and went their separate ways. As soon as the house was empty, Dani headed for the library. She retrieved the diary and continued reading.

January 18, 1894

Bernard, my beloved bulldog, and I returned from exploring in the eastern woods on the property. My curious pet discovered an old springhouse that hasn't been used for decades. It will make a good storage area for me to hide my easel and paints from my father. His hostility toward my painting has not lessened. I despise his callousness toward Bernard.

February 2, 1894

There were deer, a fawn, and a doe resting in the ravine. I was able to sketch them quickly, and I may paint them later. I also spotted a flock of turkeys but Bernard scared them away into the meadow. Their proud parading would have made a beautiful canvas. Bernard outran the male turkey who turned and strutted toward him. It was comical. Mother used to talk to me of the splendor of the forest. But she's gone.

Sarah Wythe confided to me today that she found unposted letters of Mother's meant for Da in England. Sarah said the letters were sad. I wonder why they were never posted.

February 9, 1894

Today was colder. I found a rocky stream that I sketched. I can paint the scene highlighting a winter canvas with trees bare of their leaves and snow-covered slippery stones blanketed with snow. I miss Bernard. This gentle beast disappeared. He's been gone for days.

March 11, 1894

I am devastated. Father announced his plans to have me live in Philadelphia apprenticed to one of his shipping magnates. Sarah was upset, like Mother used to be with Father's proclamations.

I shall miss Sarah. She questioned me about my beloved Bernard. I don't know why.

April 14, 1894

Father returned from Philadelphia today. Formal arrangements are set for me. I leave in two weeks. I've tried to resist, but he is relentless. I have no choice. He does not care if it makes me unhappy to follow in his business rather than be an artist.

June 3, 1894

While strolling along the river, I encountered a group painting. They are students of Professor Anshutz, who instructs at the Pennsylvania Academy of Art and Design. They paint outdoors on Saturdays.

June 10, 1894

A marvelous miracle happened. I brought a sketch and a piece of my work, and Professor Anshutz praised it. He's invited me to join their group each week along the Schuylkill.

February 4, 1895

My pure joy is painting each week with the Group of Ten. Professor has shown me how to manipulate paint to suggest light and shadows.

April 4, 1895

I had a post from Father. I've been invited home for a visit and allowed to paint while there. He is acknowledging my efforts in working at my apprenticeship.

June 15, 1895

I am returning home. I've been doing an excellent job, so it comes as no surprise to me. It appears, however, that I am not to take over the

shipbuilding. Perhaps Father reconsidered and has
agreed to my pursuit of art as a career.

Dani sighed. She could feel Nathan's loneliness and rejection
through his diary entries.

"I wonder where his canvases were kept." She looked at Riley,
who just snorted.

Voices in the hall made her rush to return the diary. Her dad
would be finishing his day.

Reaching up on the shelf where her dad put Nathan's diary,
she bumped a book and a photo album fell to the floor. Pictures
spewed everywhere. She could see Nathan, Bernard, and the vile-
looking old man who appeared in her room last night.

"Curious. Look, Riley, the three of them together."

"Dani?" She could hear him coming down the hall. She
scrambled to pick up the pictures and hid them and the album
under the couch.

He came into the library and announced, "I have a surprise."

"Hi. What surprise?"

"I thought we might take some time for R and R."

"R and R—what's that?" She smiled at him.

Hugging her, he related, "I'm done for the day, and it's still
early. How about we head on over to Mercer Museum and see
what the new exhibit holds? I can think of no better place to
soothe your mind."

Um, yeah, Dad, but you know Madisen and I already saw it."
If he asked questions about it, he would know she lied.

"That's okay. I'd like to spend time together. You've seen it, so
you can share your opinions with me. We can discuss. Besides those
exhibits can be seen over and over, like reading a good book, right?"

"Um, sure." Dani was happy to be with him, but she had to
be very careful.

Being a Saturday, the Mercer Museum was mobbed. The interactive display appealing to young people was Dani's favorite. She ran from one to the other trying out each, just like the children for whom they were meant. After three quarters of an hour, Dad suggested they move on.

Dad pressed the elevator for the third floor instead of the fourth. They exited and bumped into Rayna from the Historical Society Library.

"Hi, Dani, Nice to see you again. Didn't expect to see you so soon."

"Oh, uh, hi, Rayna." Dani stuttered, trying to conceal information from her dad. "Yes, you too." She tugged Dad away from the elevator.

"Who was that, honey, and why didn't you introduce us? What did you mean by that?"

"Oh, uh, we were here on a field trip once, and we met her." Dani had lied again, hating herself, but she wasn't ready to divulge anything until she had more facts.

"Oh, look, the library is open. I'd like to check it out." They went inside, and Dad spoke to someone in charge while Dani looked around. She itched to do more research, but she couldn't with Dad here.

Out of the corner of her eye, she saw a filmy apparition appear. The demon old man with icy eyes appeared and shouted, "Beware!"

She turned to run and tripped over her two feet. Stumbling forward, she crashed into a potted plant, disturbing the silence of the room and causing all eyes to fall on her.

"Dani, for heaven's sake, be careful." Dad reached out to take hold of her. "You're shaking as if you've seen a ghost. This old museum may have been too much for you."

As her dad assisted her back to the car, Dani became angry.

The demon is trying to scare me away from finding out more to help Nathan. I can't let him, no matter how much he threatens.

Later that night, back at the manor, she waited her chance to get the diary and take it to her room to read. Her allegiance to Nathan was becoming stronger than her fear of disobeying her dad. With everyone asleep in the house and Dani in the quiet of her room, she skipped to the final entry.

October 31, 1896

> I spent my day painting in the meadow—brilliant finches, bluebirds, nuthatches, and occasionally wild canaries. My friends at the art academy call painting outside, "plein air." I've always painted outside; I didn't know it had a name. I need to store my art somewhere else.
>
> Last night I had to dine with Father and his boorish guests. Sarah prepared a sumptuous selection of duck, venison, wild turkey, and her special vegetables. Her berry tarts and apple pies were exceptional. Her repast made the evening tolerable for me. Sarah keeps asking about Bernard. He appears to have run away.

Dani put her finger in the diary. Poor Nathan—no mother, a horror of a man for a father, and no friends. Except maybe he was building some friendships among the painters he met.

"I would hate it if my dad and I fought all the time." She looked at Riley, and he snorted in agreement. "And I hope Bernard returns. He's the only friend that Nathan has."

Giving no more thought to Bernard and considering a thought that Nathan wrote, Dani rose from the bed and went into the huge hallway. Whimpering, Riley slunk behind.

"Come on, Riley. Let's have a look in that tower room." Riley did a downward dog yoga-type move and whined. *If Nathan was looking for a new storage place, perhaps he used the tower room.*

A roar of thunder anchored Dani. A greenish glow swirled at the end of the hall, pulling her toward it like a magnet. Nathan shouted for it to "be gone," but it remained steadfast, summoning Dani. Riley growled ferociously, but it wouldn't be deterred.

"It's pulling me. I can't get out of its grip," Dani cried. Dani found herself at the foot of the stairs leading to the tower room. The boards were gone, and she could see Nathan now in front of her, at the top of the tower stairs. She seemed to fly up the staircase and into the room. Behind Nathan, a large package was illuminated in a bright light under the open attic eaves. Dani shrieked in terror as the demonic old man appeared, and Nathan turned and roared at him, "Be *gone!*"

"Dani, Dani."

A splintering noise reverberated in her head, and from somewhere far off, she could hear her dad calling her name.

"Oh, what happened? Where am I?" Dani tried to sit up in her bed. Dizziness made her fall back on her pillow.

"Riley brought us to you. We found you blacked out at the base of the door leading to the tower room." Irene's soothing tone comforted her, but her dad's constrained rapid-fire questioning made her shiver again.

"What were you doing on the fourth floor, Dani? There's no electricity up there and boards with nails all over the place. Why would you even go there?"

Dani heaved a sigh, determined to trust him and tell him the truth. "Please listen until I'm finished, Dad."

He sat on the bed and put his arms around her. "I'm listening."

"You have to believe me. Remember, you always said, 'Just because you can't prove something doesn't mean it isn't so.'"

Irene put a hand on Ray's shoulder.

Dani continued. "Nathan appeared. Then the demon came and pulled me toward the stairs or something else did. The door was open to the tower, and the boards were gone. There was a package in the tower; it was shining as if it was lit up. I know Nathan wanted me to find it."

Dad sighed and stood up. Hands on hips, then scratching

his head, he looked at Dani. Then he sat down on her bed again. "What is it you think this Nathan wants from you?" Dad's words were meticulous and slow.

"I'm not sure. I know he wants me to find something. He wants me to read his diary. I know it all has something to do with the stained glass window. I read some of it. I think the demon who haunts me is Nathan's father. His father was a nasty man, and Nathan hated him."

"I think there must be something in the tower," her dad offered.

"You do?"

"Yes, Dani. Why would he have you follow him there? I'm getting a hammer and some tools and having a look up there. It's the only way to get to the bottom of what's happening here."

"Oh, Dad, I love you." But her dad's next reply put a pin in her short-lived happiness.

"I love you too, honey. We'll check the place out, and it'll be all over."

He doesn't believe me. He's going up there to prove that I'm wrong."

Irene hugged Dani. "I feel there's something here, dear. We'll solve the mystery."

She'd tried to soothe her, but it wasn't working. She sat on edge until about a half hour later, when her father returned from the tower room.

"Dani, sometimes we think we see things that aren't there. I searched all over those eaves in the tower room. There is nothing even remotely resembling a package. In fact, the room is bare."

"That's just not possible, Dad. I saw a package glowing under the roof space. You have to believe me." Eyes welling with tears, Dani looked from her dad to Irene.

"Look, I think you're tired and overwhelmed with things that have been happening. I've made an appointment for you to talk to a professional and good friend of Dr. Robin. I'm sure she will listen and perhaps be able to explain some things. We'll see her tomorrow."

"You're wrong, Dad. There's nothing wrong with me." But now Dani's every protest sounded more like a whimpering child who was crazy."

"Dani, please." Ray tried to put his arms around her, but she fled.

Dani flailed at him. "Leave me alone."

CHAPTER 20

An Abandoned Cottage

Dani awoke refreshed but still disheartened. She had a strong compulsion to do whatever she could to help Nathan, no matter what her dad thought. She had a plan up her sleeve, but she needed the right moment to present it.

She sat down to the breakfast table, and both her dad and Irene looked at her oddly.

Dani, Irene thinks we should all read the diary, research the property, and see if we get anywhere. We'll see if anything comes to light to solve this."

I knew it. She knows more about all this.

"I'm willing to do what I can to help alleviate everyone's anxiety, including my own," he concluded.

Dani ran and hugged him. "Thank you. I'm sorry about last night. I feel like I have a responsibility to Nathan. He chose me to help him, and I feel like I've failed."

"You are very brave and caring. You could never be a failure. And whoever this spirit is, *if* he is a ghost, he doesn't deserve you," he said.

"But I think he does. That's just it. Read his diary."

Dad took the diary and went to the library. Irene went to the library in the Mercer Museum. Dani told them that she was Googling information, but she was not. They planned to spend the morning gathering facts.

When they returned, Dad began. "I'm almost finished reading the diary, but we can begin piecing some information together."

"Dad, I have something I would like to show you and something to ask you about—alone. Is that okay, Irene?"

"Of course. I'll make some soup and sandwiches so we don't starve while we share." She smiled and disappeared into the kitchen.

"What is it, Dani? What? What are you being so serious about? You're scaring me," Dad said.

Dani tried to smile. "I searched the tower room while you were gone." She produced a rolled-up item. "This is an oil canvas. It's signed N. Hainsworth."

"Dani ...," her dad started to say. She stopped him.

"And remember the box of dusty old papers that fell from a cabinet when we were in the basement, packing the town house?"

"Yes," he said hesitantly.

"They were Mom's, weren't they? Mom believed in the occult and supernatural. Didn't she?"

"Years ago, when your mom and I were first married, I learned that she had a gift. I tried to deny it, but as time passed, I realized that it was true. I think you have that gift. She knew I didn't like it, and I didn't encourage it, so she never talked about it. That was wrong of me and it's wrong now."

They sat on the sofa in the library, and he proceeded. "Your mom had a sense of super perception. Sometimes she knew things before they happened. She had an exceptional amount of insight into things that were not always clear to me or others."

"You mean that she could read your mind?"

He laughed. "Well, not quite. I can't explain exactly, but she knew things before they happened. I've come to believe that you have this gift and perhaps that's why this boy ghost is contacting you."

"Dad, you believe me."

"Yes, Dani and I should have been honest with you way before now. I'm sorry, sweetheart. I hope you'll forgive me. I have concerns. People in our society are not often supportive of differences. Your mom was different. That didn't make her crazy. Some years ago, her psychic abilities would have placed her at risk. She and I kept that a secret."

Dani threw her arms around him. "I'm so happy you believe me. Of course I forgive you. I really want to help Nathan."

"I didn't tell you because I thought you were too young and I didn't want you to be burdened by it like your mother had been. You see, sometimes it's a gift, but other times it can be, well, overwhelming."

"At least I know I'm not crazy." Dani laughed.

Irene arrived with sandwiches in the library. "How do we want to do this sharing information? I think a combination of discussion and note cards might fit the bill."

"Sounds like a good plan, ladies." Ray took a bite of his ham and swiss and chewed while listening to Dani.

"The manor has a connection to the stained glass window. Josiah Hainsworth had a chapel built on the east wing, and the piece was installed to commemorate the death of his only son, Nathan."

A booming noise thundered through the library. The chandelier swung back and forth and the dark, heavy drapes flew open. The room went icy cold, and darkness prevailed.

"*Liar!*" bellowed a throaty male voice.

Dani jumped up from the sofa and sprang into his arms. "Dad!" she exclaimed.

"Oh my goodness!" shouted Irene.

The chill remained while a filmy white apparition screeched, "Unlock the secret!"

"We can hardly unlock anything if you're going to scare us to death!" Dani cried.

As if by magic, the icy tone of the room was gone and a peaceful warmth ensued.

The three searched each other's faces for their next move.

"Obviously, we've upset someone with our findings," Dad said.

"So what part of that does the spirit object to hearing?" Irene asked. "Hainsworth Mansion was in my family. I don't know anything about the stained glass window or why the chapel was constructed. I do remember my grandparents discussing a tragedy that occurred. I believe the local authorities were involved and they suspected foul play of some sort, but I didn't know the facts. The rumor revolved around children, and that's why I was so fearful for you, Dani. I was frightened when all these strange apparitions began."

"The last date in the diary is the date on the stained glass window. What do you suppose is the meaning of that, Dad?" As she spoke, she glanced over at the stained glass window, looking harmless now, against the wall in the library. "Nathan talked about how much he loved painting," Dani suddenly blurted out. "The easel and paint tins. I forgot all about them."

"What easel?"

"I found them in the springhouse. That must be what he wants us to find. He was a painter. The bundle in the tower room. His paintings! The ghoulish old man must be Nathan's father. He never wanted Nathan to paint, and he doesn't want us to find his paintings. That must be the secret that Nathan wants us to expose."

"The stained glass window is the medium, Dani. Nathan can contact you through it. You're his recipient." Irene was clearly excited.

"But how did you get involved, Irene? You didn't know my dad, and you didn't know about the stained glass window. Or did you? Did you know that we had the piece? What made you contact my dad?" Dani was pushing with her questions.

Irene's lip quivered. "You're right, Dani. I have been keeping something because I was afraid."

Her dad directed his attention to Irene while Dani mused. *This is what I feared. Irene is somehow involved—and not in a good way.*

"I need you to trust me now. Will you both come with me? Please?"

They agreed and headed to the door. It was locked tight.

Dad pulled, tried to turn the handle, and then he pulled again. "What? Is this door stuck? It won't open."

"Unlock the secret!" a voice boomed.

"Oh dear." Irene hugged Dani.

"Let's look in the photo album. Maybe we'll find a clue." Dani went to the bookcase and quickly paged through it, coming to the section marked "Chapel."

"Look at the stained glass window hanging in the chapel. This piece is connected to this house."

There was a clicking sound, and the doorknob slowly opened.

"Let's go." Irene said. "We have some digging to do."

"Where are we going?" Ray asked. Dani thought Dad was a little too calm and didn't seem to mind at all that Irene had kept information from them and was now taking them somewhere in her car.

"Bear with me, please." Irene drove them down a grass-covered old drive that became a narrow dirt lane to the end of her property.

"This *looks* like it, but it looks so different from last month." She put hand to her head in hopelessness.

"Irene, please. What are you trying to tell us? This is becoming frustrating."

"This cottage is where I was summoned. I mean, I felt compelled to come here. It didn't look abandoned and dilapidated as it does now. Flowers were blooming, and the whole place was bright and delightful. The paint wasn't peeling as it is now. The white picket fence was covered with a vine of beautiful red roses. There were two wooden rockers with pretty blue striped cushions. I'm telling you, it was darling. And now it looks like it aged one hundred years." Tears filled Irene's eyes, "I don't understand."

Dani looked at the wooden fence with the gate falling off. "It does looks like *years* of neglect. It's scary how things are one minute and so different the next."

"I had tea here. A charming fellow in his middle years invited me in to chat. He said he lived on the property and had for some time. He said he was born here. I made a note to check on it, but it slipped my mind. I hadn't been here that long, and I'd never really been down to this end. I could hardly argue with him since I had no facts. He told me about you and said I should contact you to restore the property. I put the ad in the paper because I felt weird about calling you out of the blue. I thought if you answered the ad, it was meant to be. But then all these strange things started happening with Dani."

"Then where is he, Irene? Why does this place look like no one has lived here for years?"

"Dani, get back here," Dad called to her as she walked through the gate and up to the door of the little house.

"Are you sure you didn't get turned around, Irene. Maybe you went to a cottage down another lane on the opposite end of the property?"

Dani knocked on the door as Riley sniffed and pawed it. The door squeaked open.

"Dani, don't go in there. Let me in front here." Ray passed Irene, Dani, and Riley and stepped into the house. The others trailed behind.

"Nothing in here but dust and cobwebs. This is on your property, Irene. We aren't trespassing, so let's look around for clues to the person living here."

"Look." Dani held up another diary without initials. "This might be helpful. Can we take it with us?"

"I don't see why not," Irene said. "It could hold clues."

They moved through the place one step at a time, not knowing what they were searching for or why.

In the only bedroom, Dani found a bundle of age-worn letters tied with a burgundy ribbon. *I might need these.* She pocketed them without permission.

"I appreciate your honesty, even if it came so late, Irene. It somewhat helps explain our connection. Did that man identify himself to you and say why he recommended me?"

Before Irene could answer, Dani squealed. "Look." She pointed at a portrait of a man, a bulldog, and a small boy. "That's definitely the bulldog I keep seeing. Maybe that's a young Isaiah Hainsworth, Nathan's father. He has the same steel-gray eyes."

Her dad took the picture down and began examining it. "The back says Josiah Hainsworth."

"That's him. That's the man who advised me to hire you."

They returned to the manor, and all retreated to the library. Dani thought Irene was in some kind of trance. She'd hardly talked all the way back, and Ray even drove.

Dani was the first to break the silence. "Josiah … Isaiah, whoever, found a recipient through Irene. She's the first from the family to come here and open the house, maybe unearthing some locked powers. He's a nasty, dangerous man, and he wants to hurt Nathan."

Irene found her voice. "I'm inclined to believe Dani. I've had terrible feelings of impending doom ever since my husband and I moved in here. He was the one who wanted to restore the place.

He fell in love with it, so I went along to make him happy. But now … I think we should forget all this and leave the place."

"Irene, how did your husband die?" Dani asked.

"Heart attack. I found him in the destroyed chapel. He had a look of horror on his face."

"Oh my God, Irene, you should have told us. I can't stay here and put Dani's life in jeopardy."

"No!" Dani's shout surprised even herself. "We can't leave. Nathan needs us. Please. Let's not give up on him. Please, Dad."

"I'm going to finish reading the diary," Dad said.

"I'm going to go through the rest of the information I got from the Bucks County Historical Library. I need to read through it."

"Please … I need to lie down," Irene pleaded, leaving for her room.

"How are you doing, Dani, with all this?" He put his arm around her shoulder.

"I admit I was scared, Dad, but knowing you believe me and you're on my side helps a lot. All I want to do now is save Nathan so he can rest at peace."

In her room, Dani spread all the copied documents out and began to sift through them. She read and made notes. Reading on, she became confused as to what she was finding.

"Wait, what? I don't get this. I'm going to have to get Dad and Irene to look at this now, Riley."

A loud bellowing signaled from the hall, and an icy chill enveloped the room.

"The demon," she said to Riley, who growled ferociously and jumped back and away from the door.

The door opened on its own, and Riley escaped.

"Oh no. Come back here, Riley." She grabbed for him, but it was too late. The dog raced toward an eerie green light in the hall, following it toward the third floor stairwell. Dani had no choice but to pursue her dog.

"He's luring him to the tower room." There were no boards blocking the stairwell. Dani could see all the way up into the brightly lit tower room. She climbed the stairs in pursuit of Riley and entered the room.

Dani was so sure the mean spirit was behind this latest occurrence that she stood ready to confront him. After a short wait, it appeared that she was alone with Riley. The energetic canine sniffed around then pushed passed her, drawn to a radiant glow emanating from a spot under the eaves.

"What do you have, Ri?" She moved toward the brilliance.

"Oh my, there's a package here—quite a large, heavy thing. I can't imagine that Dad didn't see this. We need to go get him to see what's in here." Dani pulled her shirt tightly around her. "Oh, it's freezing in here."

The room began to move, and Nathan appeared. "You found my paintings, Dani. Take them quickly." Nathan's calming voice comforted her. He smiled and gestured for her to follow him toward the paintings.

All the space under the eaves was empty. "Your fault!" Nathan shouted at her.

"No, I'm trying to help. The demon must have taken them," Dani tried to explain, but Nathan raised the ax in his hand and headed toward her.

CHAPTER 21

An Incredible Find

D ani heard Dad and Irene break down the boards to the tower room staircase, rush up the steps, and bang on the door. She ran to it and unlocked it. She fell into her dad's arms.

"There wasn't anything preventing Riley and me from coming up here—no boards, no locked door." She sobbed. Dani tearfully explained how the demon summoned Riley and she followed her pet into the tower.

"There was a package hidden here, Dad." Dani pointed to where it had been. "Nathan said that I found his paintings. Then that horrible ghostly monster came and the paintings were gone. Nathan thought I had something to do with it." Shivering and crying again, she was trying to be brave but knew she was scared to death. "Please, Dad, let's try to find it. It's here somewhere. That's what Nathan wants. He needs us to find the package."

"All right, sweetheart. I'm just ecstatic that you're safe. I want this nightmare to be over, so I'll agree to another tower room search."

"Will you be okay here with Irene? I need to get some tools."

Dad looked to Irene and back at Dani. Both nodded. "I'll be as quick as I can."

He returned in a matter of minutes, and both assured him there were no further eerie incidents.

Dad surveyed the area and started pulling boards off the eaves in the spot where the parcel was seen. Nothing. He pulled off every piece of wallboard, but to no avail. "I'm sorry, honey. There doesn't seem to be anything in this tower room."

"I'm sorry too, Dad. I was so sure."

"Let's leave it alone for today. Perhaps Nathan can be more specific tomorrow." Irene was trying to be amusing, but Dani was too tired and shaken for laughter. They started toward the staircase.

"Come on, Riley. We're going down now. Ri, come." The golden retriever was interested in sniffing some floorboards, digging at them with his nails. He snarled and whined, not willing to obey Dani.

"Dad, what's he doing? He doesn't disobey." On cue, Riley barked to summon Dani.

The three went over to the floor, where he had pulled up a piece of board.

"What's this? Looks like an animal fur wrap. No, it's a package, a big one." Dad continued pulling the board off. "Hand me my hammer, please." Seconds later, he unearthed a huge bundle.

"Dad, open it here—lay it out on the floor."

Dad let out a low whistle. "Look at this."

"Oh my goodness." Irene drew her hand to her face.

"Let's get this downstairs so we can see what's in here." Ray carried the huge parcel down to the library.

"Dani, I may not be able to wrap my head around all the bizarre happenings here, but I can tell you one thing. You were *dead-on* about this artwork. Look at all these marvelous oil paintings. There must be a hundred canvases. I don't believe I ever heard of a Nathan Hainsworth who was an artist. These look very much like Bucks County impressionist oils. He must have kept this a secret from the art world."

"This is *the secret*. Nathan's secret. This is what he wanted me to reveal." Dani beamed. The three sat together in the library, recovering from their shock.

Irene appeared pensive. "This doesn't make sense, Dani. What is Isaiah's part in all this? Why keep Nathan's paintings hidden?"

"Isaiah was a horrible father, Irene. He didn't want Nathan to paint, and he certainly wouldn't have wanted Nathan to be a good and famous artist."

"I guess you're right, dear." Irene shook her head, not totally convinced.

Dani didn't care. She was thrilled that she had solved the mystery and now Nathan could rest and the demon would never return to haunt her or Riley.

"I have a good friend, Adam James. He's a very bright person and curator at Michener Museum. I'm going to call him to take a look at these. He can help us figure out what to do with them and report if there's any historical significance."

Dani waited on the marble stairs the next day. A small black spot moved up the drive. "He's here!" she shouted through the opened entry door.

The black spot moved closer and revealed a Porsche 911. Mr. Adam James exited the sports car.

"Adam, thank you so much for coming." Dad extended his hand.

"My pleasure. I'm excited to hear about your 'find.'" Adam shook Dad's hand and smiled.

Dad made the introductions and led them into the massive dining hall.

"Dani is really the one responsible for finding these. I'm afraid it seems there's a bit of the supernatural surrounding this story. I'll let Dani fill you in on the details."

"Good. I love a ghost story." Adam laughed and then was almost knocked over by Riley, who had come barreling into the room. "Oh, this must be Riley. I understand your golden retriever is your partner—or more like cohort in crime, eh Dani?"

Dani related the events from buying the stained glass to finding the paintings. When she was finished, Adam sat with a serious look.

Dad piped up. "Adam, not everyone would embrace the details of how these paintings came about. I would appreciate your confidence on these matters. I mean, the very idea of ghosts is a bit out there."

Both Irene and Dani rolled their eyes.

"My dad is embarrassed about being labeled a "believer." Dani remarked, arms akimbo.

"Yes, yes, we want to appear credible, so having us led by a spirit to his paintings after emerging himself from a hundred-year-old stained glass window would hardly make us look anything but foolish." Irene smiled and winked.

"I heartily disagree. Some spirits cannot rest until their mission is accomplished. It sounds like Nathan was not going to stop haunting until you found his paintings, Dani. But not to worry—I will not speak of that in public." Mr. James winked back at Irene.

"Let's head to the dining room and have a look," Dad suggested.

Most of the canvasses were laid out on the huge old dining room table. The bright light from the massive crystal chandelier helped to illuminate the works, but Adam had his own lighting equipment and ocular devices.

Mesmerized, Dani watched as Adam went over every inch of several paintings. Every now and then, he would scrape a tiny piece of paint or use his monocle to have a closer look.

He took an exorbitant amount of time, and Dani found herself hopping from foot to foot so much that Dad suggested she and Riley wait outside.

"I get it," she whispered. "I can't wait. I'll be still." He smiled at her, nodding his head in agreement.

"I believe." The sound of Adam's voice startled them. "Oh, sorry to frighten." He held his hand under his chin and continued. "These paintings are very old and very beautiful. They are of excellent quality work and representative of the time period, consistent with the New Hope Art Colony and their style."

He pointed to a particular oil of a winter scene. "You'll notice these tightly woven brush strokes with a multitude of colors. Indeed, they are much like the art of Garber, Lathrop, Redfield, Baum, and others. Not to mention the subject matter, all Bucks County fields, streams, and meadows, many of which I recognize. I'd need to take them to a proper authenticator with the most up-to-date technology in order to do an actual appraisal."

"Certainly, we knew you would," Dad offered.

Irene, who had been silent during all this, spoke up. "We would be so grateful, Mr. James. I can attest to the fact that many of them are paintings of trees, streams, gardens, and meadows right on this property. In addition, there are a great many not laid out here that are scenes from Philadelphia in the late eighteen nineties—the Schuylkill and Delaware Rivers and parts of Fairmount Park."

"So the paintings have historical significance as well since some of the bridges, barns, and old farms in them aren't even around anymore." Dani was proud of herself for offering this input.

Irene moved to brush a lock of hair back off Dani's forehead.

"My goodness, Nathan would be so pleased with your art knowledge, dear."

"Yes, they are a big part of Bucks County history, and you can't put a price on that if they are indeed original oils and we establish that. Due to the historical perspective, quality of the work and obvious connection to the Bucks County impressionists, if what you tell me from the diary is correct and can be authenticated, then we are looking at millions of dollars. Some of these pieces may be worth a million or at least a half a million each."

Dani couldn't quite imagine that amount of money. She looked at Irene and her dad, and the looks on their faces agreed with hers.

"I'm speechless." Dad admitted. "I wasn't expecting that. Yes, they're beautiful, but it's starting to sink in what we have here."

"This is about the biggest news to hit Bucks County art world in quite some time. It will change your lives—I'll tell you that. I'd try to keep a lid on it until you figure out your next moves. I'll gather up my tools and get a call into the gallery in town. They've done several famous authentications, so they have great credentials. I'll see if they can get a team out here ASAP. I would also advise you to get some security, folks, maybe an attorney and your insurance company."

"Nathan will be so pleased. He'll finally be where he belongs in the proper place in the art world history." Dani's eyes filled.

"He owes it all to you, Dani." Irene hugged her.

"Oh, yeah, about that. Nathan Hainsworth may not be so enthralled with you, Dani."

Dani stopped smiling through her tears. "What do you mean, Mr. James?"

"Nathan Hainsworth did not paint these paintings."

They stood there, stunned.

CHAPTER 22

Notable Notes

Dani pondered Adam's words while she watched her dad walk him to his car.

"Irene, could you drive me to the library at the Mercer Museum? I'm shocked, and I need to research something myself."

Dani spent the next few hours at the library and then gathered her tablet and pushed in her chair. She sighed, wondering aloud, "Can Nathan explain this to me?"

They agreed to table any talk of ghosts and diaries over dinner. Dani was exhausted by her emotional day and begged to go to sleep early. She fell asleep quickly.

The sound of whispers followed by an icy chill roused her from sleep. Booming noise thundered through her bedroom. Nathan appeared to be trying to materialize at the foot of her bed. His filmy image disappeared. The demon appeared in her room holding the nameless diary that she found in the abandoned cottage. He held it up toward her, letting it fall. He was gone. The cold air returned to warm, and her room was quiet again.

"What does he want? Riley, this book was in the demon's

possession." Shivering but more curious than scared, she began reading this new log. It was after midnight, but Dani kept reading, becoming more distraught after each entry. She closed the book, her heart full of sadness.

Dani looked at the clock. It was four thirty. She had tossed and turned for several hours and then couldn't continue. Remembering the pack of letters that she also found in the cottage, she dug them out of her bureau and began to peruse through them.

June 15, 1886

My dearest father,
The pastels arrived, and Jonathan couldn't contain his excitement. Even at his young age, he demonstrates an enormous talent for observing and detailing beautiful pictures on paper. He has your artistic ability. Josiah and I support and praise his work. He's a sweet lad and wishes to see you again.

The letter went on, but Dani was becoming confused. Who wrote it? She skipped to the end. It was signed, *Lovingly, your daughter, Katherine.*

"Who was Katherine?" Dani looked at Riley. She scanned the last paragraph.

Josiah and I are still very much concerned about our precious, Nathan. Josiah and I dote on both brothers, but Nathan is a willful child and continues to torment and hurt his twin. Pray for all of us, Father.

It was becoming clear to Dani, but she was horrified and

didn't want to read further. *No, this can't be true. This must be Nathan's mother, Katherine. I'm so mixed up. This isn't like the entries in Nathan's diary. I can't tell Irene and Dad about this. Nathan has a right to explain.* She was about to put the letters back in the drawer when a frigid breeze engulfed her. She looked up to find Nathan, not with soulful, gentle eyes but with eyes intense with hatred. A ball of fire leaped onto the letters.

"Oh no, please don't destroy them." Dani stomped her foot on them and folded the small rug over them.

Nathan outstretched his arm, willing her to follow. Dani breezed down the stairs on air and reached the library. She was too terrified to speak. Nathan turned to face her. Dani found her voice.

"We found your paintings, Nathan, and my dad was ready to display them and tell the world about you."

He smiled, but not the innocent sweet smile she was used to seeing. Her teeth chattered as she realized this was the first time she didn't trust Nathan.

"Nathan," Dani said, summoning her courage, "I need you to answer some questions."

Nathan turned to the stained glass window, which now was alive, with colors swirling in and around it.

"Answer." A thundering roar followed by a whirling dervish of black, green, and purple flames filled the library. The old man demon appeared from within them, bellowing for Nathan's response.

"Get out—go away!" Dani shrieked, but to no avail. The booming noise and hideous vision remained. "What do you want?"

The apparition held the journal that Dani found in the cottage. He flung it to the floor and bellowed, "Truth!"

Nathan lunged at the apparition, and they both disappeared.

"Riley, the book and the letters ... Something is terribly

wrong. Those letters have to be fakes. The demon is preventing Nathan from getting the credit he deserves." Dani perused the rest of the letters and the book. She became more agitated as she read. The sound of her dad and Irene in the kitchen roused her.

"Guys, I have to show you something," Dani said. "I found these in the little cottage at the end of the property. I'm confused." After sharing the book with Dad and the letters with Irene, Dani and Riley snuggled on the sofa and waited for answers.

Dad was the first to speak. "This diary belonged to Isaiah Hainsworth, Dani. He was Josiah's twin. I'm afraid there are some nasty accusations in here." He read a few passages to them.

January 4, 1894

I've had some very tragic news from my brother Josiah and my sister-in-law, Katherine. My brother fears for his life, his wife's, and his young son, Jonathan. He is torn for his love of his twin boys, one a monster.

Looking up, Dad cleared his throat, a pained expression on his face. He picked out another entry.

April 11, 1894

I am leaving for America. My brother Josiah and Katherine, his wife, are missing, as is their son, Jonathan. Authorities are investigating. I will take charge of Josiah's business affairs and care for my nephew, Nathan.

"Then the man Nathan calls *father* in his diary is really his uncle Isaiah. No wonder he hated him." She thought for a moment. "But that doesn't explain anything. Why did he hate him? And why did he call him *father*?" Dani was afraid of what they were going to find out. Her eyes teared, and her stomach clenched tight, betraying her feelings for Nathan.

Dad continued through the diary, skipping entries and focusing on relevant ones.

April 14, 1894

I am deeply saddened. My nephew is terribly ill, and it's not a physical illness. I have alerted local authorities, and they are pursuing a special investigation into my brother's disappearance. The boy needs to be hospitalized in the city. I do this as a last resort and with a heavy heart.

"Dad, wait. Before you continue ..." Dani went to the bookcase to retrieve Nathan's diary. She opened to the exact dates that coincided with the dates from Isaiah's diary and read them to her dad and Irene.

"My goodness, how confusing. Who can make sense of all this?" Irene sighed.

"Nathan's accounting in his diary matches the entry dates but not the content. Keep reading, Dad." Dani's anxiety increased at every entry.

June 3, 1894

The authorities have found no clues after a continued search. Nathan is faring well. He is in a clinical trial and responding to new medications. He is permitted to be outside for fresh air on occasions. I pray for his recovery.

Clutching at any hope she could find, Dani announced, "Maybe Nathan was delirious from those medications and confused about what he was writing." She shot a hopeful look at Irene and her dad.

June 15, 1895

My heart is heavy. Authorities found the skeletons of my brother, Katherine, and Jonathan in the old abandoned springhouse.

"That's horrible." Dani clenched her fists to her face, whispering, "Poor Nathan. His whole family murdered. Read on, Dad. Does it say anything else?"

Dani was holding Nathan's diary, flipping the pages from front to back, when a page flew to the floor. "Wait, what's this? The entry is October thirty-first. The rest isn't here. Maybe it fell out."

"Read it, Dani."

Father is furious with me and threatens to sell Bernard and send me to Philadelphia permanently. I must run away at once and take Bernard with me.

"Dad, read the entry in Isaiah's diary for that date."

"There isn't one. But there is one for November first." Dad read it to them, and they gasped.

"Nathan took Bernard and ran away, like he said he would. What does he want us to unlock? What about his paintings? And, Dad, why did Adam James say they weren't painted by Nathan?"

"I can answer that question. When I walked Adam to his car, he told me the initials on the paintings were NH, but they had been painted over the original signature, Jonathan Hainsworth."

Dani paled. "I don't feel well. I'm going outside to get some fresh air." Riley followed.

"I understand, honey. Don't go far and no woods."

She wished he hadn't said that, because that's where she needed to go, to the springhouse.

A short walk later, she entered the springhouse. The room was icy, leaves whirled around the window, and Dani could sense a spirit's presence. She bent over to retrieve the tin of paints next to the easel. Standing up, she noticed a package stuffed into a crevice. She pulled it out and opened it, shocked at the contents. It was a wad of canvases, all oil paintings of bright red and black. She rose to face Nathan.

"I wanted to unlock the secret, Nathan. I wanted to help you."

"*Nooo!*" a voice boomed. The ghoulish-looking demon emerged.

"He can't hurt you, Dani. Run!" a voice roared. The room filled with eerie green light.

Dani ran for the door and found herself entering the library in the mansion with Riley, both out of breath.

"Dani, what happened? You're as pale as a ghost. Oh no." Irene knew what happened. "The specters?"

"The demon tried to keep me from getting Nathan's paints. These might answer some questions." She held the tin of paints and canvases out for her dad.

He took it, frowning at her. "I said no woods. Do you ever listen to me?" He looked at the tin and oil paintings and looked up in surprise. "This just complicates matters more." He returned the tin to Dani.

"Nooo," she uttered, and a tear fell down her face.

CHAPTER 23

Final Secret Revealed

"These aren't Nathan's." She wiped the dirt from the top of the tin container, her face distraught.

"No, they aren't, Dani. The *J* has been manipulated to resemble an *N*."

"I didn't want to admit it to myself, Dad. I discovered some additional facts when I went to the Mercer library last week." Dani detailed how she found the birth certificates of identical twins Jonathan and Nathan Hainsworth, born to Josiah and Katherine Hainsworth. Between the letters Katherine wrote to her da in England and the newspaper clippings locally, Dani determined that Nathan had a mental illness.

"His mother wrote that Nathan would torture his brother, making up lies about him to get him in trouble, torture innocent animals, lie to his parents, throw tantrums, and threaten them. She said he became more violent as he grew older. His own parents feared him. They didn't know what to do. They asked for Isaiah's help. I thought he was the demon and the evil one."

"That's not the case?" Dad searched her face for a reply.

"Isaiah, the demon, came to my rescue in the springhouse. Nathan wanted to take over my soul and body to restore his life. I learned some things about Ouija boards and spirits. There are avenues they use, portals to this world. The stained glass was Nathan's portal to me."

"Hold that thought." Dad held up his hand to take a cell call in the next room.

"Dani, you rest here a minute. I'm going to brew us some tea. Then we can resume our story." Irene left Dani on the sofa to prepare tea.

A sudden intense cold filled the air. Dani stiffened. Her dad returned. A force flipped him upward and deposited him on the floor across the room.

"Stop, stop! Don't you dare hurt my father."

Nathan had tossed her father as the demon materialized. The old man, who was not a demon at all but Dani's protector, charged at Nathan. Nathan was faster than the scrawny old man, knocking him to the ground in pursuit of Dani. He raised a dagger to her.

"We know who you are, Nathan. You're not a good person. We know what you've done. Leave us alone. Leave this house." It took all the strength Dani could muster. The scent of lavender filled the room. Dani continued. "You're a bully and a liar, Nathan. You aren't an artist at all. Your brother was the genius artist, not you."

As Dani spewed her words at the ghost, he crumpled. His face shriveled into a grief-stricken pose and disappeared. The demon, Isaiah, who was not a demon at all, returned.

"He'll bother you no more, girl. He was a sick child, and it was not his fault. Demons troubled his mind. Perhaps now he can rest since the truth is known," the old man proclaimed. He then vanished, and the iciness was gone.

Dani moved to help her dad up. He had no memory of the

previous scene. "What am I doing on the floor? Did I fall?" Dad rubbed his head while leaning on Dani.

Irene returned with tea and cookies, and Dani tried to relate the bizarre details. "Isaiah was really the good guy. His brother, Josiah, became more fearful of Nathan and what he might do as he grew older. There wasn't much help for mental illness back then. He was still their son, and they loved him. They didn't want to send him away to an institution.

When Isaiah arrived, he sent Nathan to a hospital to be cured. He became a model patient, and the doctors assured Isaiah that he could be released. Nathan came home to Hainsworth Manor. Then the bodies were found. The investigation led to Nathan. Criminal charges were filed. That's when Nathan ran away."

"What became of him?" Irene was curious. "Did they find him?"

"He never returned to the manor after that last day in October. His uncle was distraught because he believed he had failed his brother and Nathan. He memorialized the day he disappeared with the stained glass." Dani paused and looked at them. "Sarah Wythe loved Nathan in spite of her fear of him. I think she may have tried to intervene for me too."

"How so, Dani?" Dad asked.

"Nathan talked a lot about her in his diary. He mentioned she wore a lavender scent. There was a lavender scent in the room when he was about to stab me but didn't."

Dad smiled. "I don't want to add false information to this tale, but your mom wore lavender too. Just saying."

"Thanks for that, Dad." Dani hugged him and then continued. "I thought Isaiah was a demon trying to hurt Nathan and keep me from locating his paintings, when all the time he was protecting me. Nathan's diary was a lie. It was Nathan's sick perception of himself and his world, but it was not reality. He wrote about being an artist and being an apprentice to a shipbuilder, when he was really in Philadelphia in a private hospital for the mentally ill."

Irene shook her head. "Nathan was a very disturbed soul, and mental illness needs more understanding and support. Perhaps if his parents had a place to go or doctors who had more knowledge, Nathan's life would have been different. And his parents and brother would have lived."

"We don't know enough, spend enough money on research, or support those with mental illnesses. We've come a long way, but we have just as far to go in this field of medicine," her dad added. "From the information we gathered, Nathan was suffering from a psychopathic disorder."

"I did research about that, Dad. Doctors haven't been able to cure it yet because the brain of a psychopath lacks neurons and has a lot of gray matter in the area of the brain that deals with emotion and behavior. They can *manage* the person using behavior-changing methods, but there's no cure and no medication."

"I do wonder what happened to him when he left the mansion. The diaries don't reference anything about that. I guess we'll never know." Dad rubbed his head in wonderment.

The next day, Adam James arrived with facts about the paintings, the artist, and notes of interest. They in turn related Dani's latest experience.

"This explains why Nathan chose you, Dani. Your closeness in age gave him a peer and a kindred spirit. You are the first young person in the mansion since his disappearance. Maybe he wanted the stained glass returned to his home."

Dani didn't hold any stock in Mr. James's theory. She thought Nathan wanted the glass returned so he could exit from it and inhabit her soul. But she didn't share that. Something was still unclear about Nathan. He had been sweet when he first appeared, and then he became nasty. She wondered if that was the nature of his disease—maybe like schizophrenia.

"The artist was Jonathan Hainsworth, not Nathan. He painted as a teen and was quite good. His parents sent him to the academy in Philadelphia. He might have been one of the Bucks County impressionists had he lived. Everything in Nathan's diary was really about Jonathan," Dani whispered, lowering her head. "The book was given to Jonathan as a going-away gift from his mother. It's in the letters Katherine wrote to her father in England. That's the difference in handwriting in some sections. Nathan tried to copy his brother's style."

Adam talked at length with her dad and Irene, and Dani hardly heard him until he said her name.

"What? Did you mention me?" Dani piped up.

"I obtained access to the contents of a vault in Isaiah's name. There might be relevant information in a letter written by Isaiah to be opened after his death. You are the next of kin now, Irene." Adam handed her the letter.

Irene looked questioningly at Adam, read the letter, and then looked up in dismay. "This is tragic. We have to call the police immediately." She handed the letter to Ray.

"What is it?" Dani looked from one to the other.

"The letter maintains that Isaiah was overcome with grief when he realized his worst fears about Nathan," Dad explained. "His nephew had indeed murdered his whole family, including his beloved Bernard. He was to be incarcerated in one of the worst asylums in the city. He was just a boy, Isaiah argued to the authorities, and the drugs were working. Nathan was making tremendous strides, but alas, it was too late. Isaiah couldn't imagine the boy incarcerated in such a horrible dismal place, so he poisoned him and disposed of his body in the old well."

"Which explains why Nathan couldn't rest." Dani sobbed.

"Nathan had already made an entry in his diary about running away. Isaiah read the boy's diary daily. No one would suspect that Isaiah had a hand in it, and he saw it as a more compassionate ending for the boy," Irene added. "There was never an investigation, and the case is still open."

Minutes later, a police car arrived and a uniformed police officer and another man in a white suit looking like a space alien got out. Her dad and Irene went out to greet them.

"Let's hang out here, Madisen," Dani said, peeking out the windows, not wanting to miss the hype. Irene and Dad stood just outside the library doors.

"It's taking forever. I wish they'd share what they're finding. Oh, here comes the coroner. Let's go outside so we can hear what she says."

"My team has retrieved two skeletons from the old well. One is believed to be a young human and the other a canine. We are transporting them to the lab. The teeth are still intact, so that will help in dating them. We'll try to use DNA polymorphism extracted from the bones. Identification may not be positive, but age should be no problem. We'll keep you updated."

Tears streamed down Dani's face. She had grown to love Nathan and Bernard and looked forward to their appearances—until recently.

"I know he was already dead, Dad, but I still feel sorry for him. He had a disease. If he had cancer, everyone would have supported and cared for him. But no one understands the mentally ill."

"Maybe someday things will change, Dani." Dad hugged her tight.

A reporter stuck a microphone right up Dani's nose and

asked, "Are you related to the bodies in the well? Care to give a statement?"

"Dad!" Dani cried.

"Enough." Dad signaled to the chief.

Chief George Casey pulled his Doylestown police cruiser closer and got out.

"Chief, could you clear the place so we can have some privacy?"

"Happy to oblige." He lifted his bullhorn and spoke through it. The media began to clear off the private property.

Later, in the library, the group of four and Riley gathered around a cozy fire.

Irene sighed. "A week ago at this time, we had no idea that we would own millions of dollars of art this week."

"It's yours, Irene, not mine or Dani's."

"I have something to confess that I've been keeping from you."

Dad and Dani did double takes. "I thought we agreed no more secrets, Irene."

Irene stood up and paced. "I was about to tell you, then things started happening and I wasn't sure where they would take us and … it just got away from me."

Dani eyed her. *I knew it. I knew she was hiding something.*

"When I met Isaiah in the cottage and had tea, he gave me a genealogy chart. He didn't explain why; he just told me to keep it safe. But we are all descendants of Matthew Hainsworth. He was the grandfather of Isaiah and Josiah."

"What does that have to do with us? I know who my great-great-grandfather was, and he *wasn't* a Hainsworth." Ray smacked his knee as if to prove it.

"No, but your wife, Regina, used the middle name Madden. She was a descendent of Bess Madden, who was married to

Matthew Hainsworth. Your wife's ancestors and mine were distant cousins of Isaiah and Josiah. I believe Isaiah knew the value of the paintings and wanted them to stay in the family."

"This is astounding, Irene. Do you have proof? Other than the ramblings of an alleged *specter*?"

"Of course I do, Ray." She smiled at Dani.

"Yeah, Dad, we have DNA for proof to satisfy the nonbelievers." This got a chuckle from all three since they knew that her dad needed solid evidence before he believed in anything.

Dani turned to Irene. "I've been thinking that it would be a great tribute to Jonathan Hainsworth if you built a gallery where the chapel used to be and exhibit his works with his story."

"Lovely idea, dear."

"And the money we charge for admission can be donated to Doylestown Hospital Behavioral Health in Nathan's name for research into mental health," Dani stated confidently.

Later that night, Dani was gathering her things into her backpack, readying for the next day. Her eye traveled to the stained glass still standing against the library wall. It twinkled and chimed, and then two figures enshrouded in white mist appeared and materialized into Nathan and his beloved bulldog.

"Isaiah," Dani whispered.

He smiled, held his hand on his heart, and departed without a word.

ACKNOWLEDGMENTS

Thank you to all my friends and family who encouraged me to continue and complete this novel.

A special thank you to Marge Ahoub, Beth Campbell, Kathy Patton, Lauren Zucker, and Sarah Olsen for reading my first drafts and offering advice. To friends Mary Zisk and Barb Massa, who were in my first critique group. To Kathy Temean, past regional director of New Jersey Society of Children's Book Writers and Illustrators, for making it possible to meet authors and take writing classes and workshops to hone my skills. To Leslie Zampetti, who along with my Avalon Retreat group, provided advice and support. To my BFF, Suzanne Brown, who always says positive words and makes me laugh; to friends Judy Michael, Pat Goodrich, Russ, and Heidi Lane for constant encouragement, and especially to Russ, for checking on my progress and pushing me forward. To my good friend and fellow author Anita Nolan, painter, editor, and teacher, who helped me learn the craft. A huge heartfelt thank you, Anita, for the valuable writing classes, reading lists of both fiction and writer's craft, and hours of direction in the revision process. And to the other members of my Book Club, thank you for all your positive support.

To my lovely daughter, Kati, who read my novel to my grandsons before bed and provided great kid feedback. To Ethan, my wonderful son, the original inspiration for the characters in the book, and to my son Jonathan for words of encouragement and gifts of writing books.

Last, but most important, to my wonderful, adoring husband, Larry, for always having my back, offering encouragement and valuable critiques, and becoming the cook, housekeeper, shopper, and reader and editor of many, many, revisions. I love you.

CPSIA information can be obtained
at www.ICGtesting.com
Printed in the USA
LVHW031223070720
659963LV00002B/219

9 781532 087264